WARNING

This book contains sexually explicit scenes and adult language. It may be considered offensive to some readers. This book is for sale to adults ONLY.

Please store your files wisely where they cannot be accessed by underage readers.

* * * * * * * * * * * * * * * * * * *

WANT FREE COPIES OF MY BOOKS?
Just visit my blog and download free copies of my books:
amy-redek.awesomeauthors.org/amy-redek

About the Publisher

4Fun Publishing, a member of **BLVNP Incorporated**, 340 S. Lemon #6200, Walnut CA 91789, info@blvnp.com / legal@blvnp.com
NOTE: Due to the highly emotional reaction of some people to works of erotic fiction, any email sent to the above address that contains foul language or religious references is automatically deleted by our anti-spam software and will not be seen. All other communications are welcome.

DISCLAIMER

Please don't be stupid and kill yourself. This book is a work of FICTION. Do not try any new sexual practice that you find in this book. It is fiction and not to be confused with reality. Neither the author nor the publisher or its associates assume any responsibility for any loss, injury, death or legal consequences resulting from acting on the contents in this book. Every character in this book is over 18 years of age. The author's opinions are not to be construed as the opinions of the publisher. The material in this book is for entertainment purposes ONLY. Enjoy.

The Square Circle

Murder is the Name of the Game
Seductive Suspense

By: Amy Redek

ISBN: 978-1-62761-807-6

DURING THE few days before Christmas, Oxford Street can be equated with a child's vision of the way it must be in Santa Claus' homeland. A blaze of coloured lights curled their way up lamp posts and crisscrossed the street to descend upon the other side. Many wove themselves into intricate patterns while some were pure advertisements. Atop each post was either Santa Claus in a sleigh or the most popular of Walt Disney's characters, such as Snow White with a couple of dwarfs.

The shops themselves were all ablaze with lights and scenes of winter wonderlands, grottoes or a few with scenes of the Nativity, still misrepresented with snow. It was the automatons that caught children's eyes and glued them to the large windows, noses pressed up tight to the glass, their breath misting the panes.

People moved at a slower pace than normal, pausing at various windows to appreciate the artistry of one, the beauty of another, appreciating the time and effort that some store employee had put in to make their display the best. If they were jostled or had toes trodden on, the apology was accepted without question and was usually followed by an offering of the season's greetings.

All were in general good humour, looking forward to the Christmas break, of the presents they give to children or loved ones, and of those that they would receive in return. The weather never deterred these people from filling the street be it rain, wind or snow, bustling up and down every year, in and out of the stores. Parcels were dropped, bags would split, and all would think it funny as they collected them up and tried to hail taxi's that were always occupied.

That is at Christmas time. The January sales are different. Though some of the lights are still on, the blown bulbs make a mockery of some of the advertising slogans. Snow White has slipped sideways so that it appears as if Happy is looking up her dress - no wonder he smiles - and Santa's sleigh appears to be making a nosedive down to the pavement. The windows of the stores are much of a muchness; all with large red printed banners announcing that there is a sale on. Twenty percent off; special discounts; nought per cent finance; buy now and pay later. The banal advertising manager has taken over from the gifted window dresser and they must have all gone to the same Art College, because it was difficult to tell when one store finished and another began.

It was a bitter wind that made the pedestrians scurry along, muffled up to their ears, red tips peeking above collars and scarves. No thoughts of stopping to look at the meagre displays, but just to get inside the overheated stores and out of the wind. Then came the cloying, tongue tasting waft of mixed perfumes being sprayed on wrists that then flap about before being put to the nose. The crowds of people moving in all directions at once, bumping and boring their way through in the direction that they think will lead them directly to the counter they are seeking.

The crush is a swirling eddy that never seems to find an outlet till one is suddenly pushed out of the stream to find the walls moving back and downwards, realising that it's an escalator taking you up to another seething cauldron of humanity. It's a pickpocket's dream and the shoplifter's heaven of bodies pressed together so fingers are unfelt and many big coats have lots of small inside pockets.

Parcels, bags, baskets are constantly hitting the knees or thighs as they swing in the tight grip of the buyer clinging to the bargain of the year. Then into the fray of quickly trying to find the hanger on the rack with the right size for you. Of course not in any semblance of order, but seeming all to be either for midgets or women who, if they were there, wouldn't be able to get through the narrow spaces left between the racks.

But with a few things that might, or look as though they will fit, the struggle comes to find the queue that never moves at a paying counter. Wait forever while the assistants, harried and stressed, try to remove the stubborn anti-shoplifting tag. They should really be trained by the professional shoplifter in this art, as they can remove them one handed while concealing them away at the same time. Then tapping into the computer the code for making up the final total, which then is paid for by credit card, which takes time to be verified before the machine agrees to let the slip of paper chunter out of its slot to be signed.

In this maelstrom of activity, four women are in these queues at different points in the store, waiting their turn, relishing the thought of sitting down for a few minutes with a cup of tea in the cafeteria on the fourth floor. Hoping against hope that there will be an empty seat so that shoes can be slipped off and the toes wiggled because they'd put on the wrong pair that morning at home.

The cafeteria, as expected, was crowded. The queue wasn't as long as Francis thought as she picked up her tray and joined the end of it. Francis Mann didn't mind the bustle of the city, coming from the small town of Malden in Essex. She had driven into Chelmsford with her husband, and they had travelled down by train that morning to London. Him to go to work while she went on this shopping expedition. Francis was just past her thirty-ninth birthday, dreading the next one, but was happy that she could still pass for a late twenty-year-old. Her figure, while not exactly hourglass, was still trim in spite of giving birth to a daughter twenty years previously. Her bust was nice and matronly and her legs were still slender that finished down at size five shoes. Ash blonde hair that didn't seem to need brushing at any time, framed a face once described as beautiful but now called very pretty. The pencilled eyebrows above soft brown eyes that had only a hint of mascara so as not to be distractive, led down to a short, but straight nose above her soft lips.

Behind her in the queue stood Penelope Swithers, though she always preferred to be known as Penny. She was only out that day because she was bored at home. Home being a house in Knightsbridge, so she hadn't travelled very far to be in the store. Penny was thirty years old and looked like a model in her trim suit having the figure that you would never see on a catwalk. Top heavy was her own description of herself, but from there down, perfect. She too was blonde, but tending more to the brunette colour than that of Francis before her in the queue. Her face was long but balanced by the wide blue eyes and generous mouth separated by her nose that on a round-faced person would have been large, but suited her perfectly.

Francis reached the till and paid for her tea, pastry and small chocolate bar, and moved off. Penny paid for her coffee, a slice of cake and a peach, and followed on through the crowded tables and nearly lost the lot when Francis suddenly stopped to turn round.

'Oh sorry,' said Francis, seeing the tray Penny was carrying, nearly tilt the contents off. 'I didn't realise anyone was behind me. This place is so full I can't see an empty seat.'

'There's an empty table over there,' Penny said, indicating with her chin across the shoulder of Francis.

'Oh you're right,' she replied after looking round, 'let's grab it quick before anyone else.'

They moved quickly between the other full tables, neatly swerving around crooked elbows and side stepping the bags and parcels that were in every little aisle. The table was in a corner and had just been vacated, but was still littered with trays and used crockery and other debris.

'Here, hold my tray a moment,' Penny said, handing her tray to Francis as they reached the table. 'I'll clear this off for us.'

Francis stood with both trays in her hands while Penny scooped all the litter onto two of the trays and looking round, but not finding anywhere they could go, gave a grin to Francis and pushed them between the two long flower troughs that bordered the eating area.

'Let them pick those up later,' she smiled, taking her tray back and sitting down. Francis pulled out a chair and setting her tray on the table, sat down opposite.

Two other women saw the table being cleared and both made a beeline for the two vacant seats that were there. The first was Anne Seymour, and apart from her hair being a soft brown, could have been the bookend for Penny, her figure being almost the same. She was big breasted above a trim waist and had long slim legs with well-rounded calves, and like Penny, was only thirty years old.

'May I join you?' she asked of Francis and Penny, standing by the table.

'By all means,' Francis replied with a slight wave of the hand, and Anne put her tray down and sat next to her.

'Can I too?' asked Jane, eyeing the last seat and having heard Anne ask the question.

'Certainly,' said Penny, removing her handbag from the last chair. With a sigh, Jane gratefully sank down on the seat beside her.

'Hi! I'm so glad to get off my feet. My name's Jane. Short for Jane,' she said with a little laugh. 'Yours?' was the query left in the air.

'Anne.'

'Francis.'

'Penny.'

'Well it's nice to meet you. I've just had a bellyful of this place. Worse than Epsom on Derby day. Bet you've never seen a crowd like this before in here?' Jane was married to a book-maker, hence her manner of speech and outgoing personality. London born and bred, she oozed the very spirit of a person raised within the sounds of Bow Bells. Short sharp pithy words and quick head movements like a pigeon constantly looking out for signs of danger. Shorter than the others, but not by much.

Again, thirty years old, but with her round face framed by her black hair at shoulder length, looked younger, except for the little lines at the corner of the eyes that only another woman would see to guess her age correctly. Her figure was slimmer than the others' and not quite in proportion having smaller breasts, thicker waist and fuller hips. Too much eating in restaurants or from hot dog stands at racetracks was not a healthy way to eat.

'It is a trifle crowded,' Anne admitted, sipping her tea, 'I only came to get out of the house for a while.'

'Me too. All day cooped up, never seeing anyone gets you really depressed,' replied Penny.

'I can spend all day in the garden and still not see a soul go past,' chipped in Francis.

'Where do you live then?' asked Penny.

'Just outside the village of Malden, in Essex,' she replied.

'An Essex girl!' sniggered Jane.

'Not at all,' Francis replied indignantly, 'I was born in Sussex. My husband was born in Essex though.'

'Do the old jokes apply to them too?' enquired Penny with a straight face, but a hint of a smile at her lips.

'I think so,' was the laughing reply, 'boring, and as much sex appeal as a lamppost,' nibbling on her pastry.

'That's the trouble with my husband. Too much sex appeal. I never see the bastard much these days,' said Penny gloomily, looking down into her empty cup. 'I wish one of his popsie's would take him off my hands. The divorce settlement would suit me down to the ground.'

'Well I see mine too much. I'm dragged from racecourse to racecourse. But then, when I don't go, I hear he has some tart with him. Yes, a divorce settlement would sort me out too!' Jane put in.

'Humph,' snorted Anne, 'if my husband saw another woman, he wouldn't know what to do. He wouldn't have the time anyway. You can set your watch by his habits. Divorce would be no good to me, he's worth more with his life insurance.'

Pushing her empty plate a little and dabbing at her lips with a tissue, Francis said, 'I'm in the same boat there, though I'm worth more dead to him than he is to me. Must sort that out one day, then maybe it would be worthwhile having him bumped off!' She gave a little hiccup. 'Oh do excuse me,' she said with a little laugh.

'I wish someone would do that for me,' Penny said wistfully.

'Kill him you mean?' asked Jane.

'Why not? He might just as well be dead for what I see of him. Besides, I wouldn't waste money like he does.'

'I don't get any money, well not much to speak of. For this shopping trip I have to use a credit card with a limit given me by my husband!' said Anne.

'That *is* the limit,' declared Jane, and then in a musing tone, 'I could take over the bookmaking and keep all the money myself. Or take in a partner. Perhaps you, Penny. Instead of his slogan, "A pound for a Pound," we could make it "In for a Penny, in for a Pound."' She laughed gaily, and the others did too.

'What about you, Anne?' asked Penny, 'No credit card limit. The sky would be the limit.'

'I don't know,' she said, absently stirring her spoon round in an empty cup before realising what she was doing, letting the spoon drop clattering into the saucer. 'It would be foolish to try. You'd be the first suspect after taking out a hefty insurance and then he's popped off. Well, you know what I mean.'

'Not if you were somewhere else and had a cast iron alibi,' Jane said. 'I mean if it looked like he died as a result of an accident.'

'I wouldn't mind if somebody else did it,' Anne popped in.

Jane gave a little flutter of her hands, indicating for the others to lean forward closer. The heads of all four moved closer to the centre of the table as she whispered, 'What if we got together and did it ourselves? Knock them off at different times, different places, and all that?'

Then they all leaned back and gave serious looks to each other, the silence around the table very deafening within the café's hubbub. Jane leaned forward again.

'Let's not say anymore on this now. What I suggest is that if we are interested, let's meet again in about a month's time, say at the wine bar next door for lunch, and then talk? Say about one o'clock?'

She looked at Penny who nodded straight away. Francis, after a slight hesitation, then at Anne, who flushed with the three pairs of eyes on her, and dropping her own eyes, slowly nodded, and so an agreed date and time was set.

'Well,' Penny said. 'As I live here in London, shall I book a table for then?'

'Good idea,' Jane replied.

'My God, is that the time!' Anne exclaimed. 'I've got to get home. He has to have his dinner on the table at exactly six fifteen.' As she grabbed at her handbag and carrier bag, Jane caught hold of her wrist.

'Think what it would be like if you didn't have to rush, ever again,' she whispered softly, slowly letting go. 'See you next month?'

'Maybe you will,' she replied, 'maybe I will see you all. Bye for now.' Then with a flurry of coat and bag, she left the table and made her way out of the café.

'I'd better make a move too,' said Jane, 'maybe I'll catch the bastard in bed with one of his tarts and do the job myself.'

'Without the insurance?' Penny asked.

'You're right! See you next month then, and, oh,' she gave a throaty chuckle, 'I forgot. There's a horse in the three forty five tomorrow. Put your shirt on it. It's hot at twenty to one.' She picked up her things and was just leaving the table.

'What's the name?' queried Francis.

"Blood Money," Jane laughed as she left.

'Well if that horse comes in I'll see it as an omen and be here next month,' Francis said, putting out her hand. Penny took it and said softly,

'See you next month.'

Ironically, the horse did win.

***

ANNE HURRIED down the escalators till she reached the ground floor, and ignoring the looks she got from the people she knocked aside, made her way out of the store. The cold wind was like a knife slicing through her open coat. She had to stop to button up, then with bags in hand, scurried to Oxford Street station. She had to make her connections or her husband Robert would be home before her and then there would be hell to pay.

She had only once been late with his dinner, and remembered it well. It had been on a Thursday during the summer and she had been having afternoon tea with the vicar and his wife at the Vicarage. A phone call came from a farm outside of the village from a Mrs. Watkins. She was hysterical but managed to get out that her husband had been in an accident on the farm and would he go out to see him. The doctor was already on his way, but the farmer was asking for him. Anne asked if she could go along to help and the vicar welcomed the offer and took her in his car.

She sat and comforted the farmer's wife and got the tea for the children when they came home from the village school, while the vicar was in with the doctor.

The vicar thanked her for her help with the family as he drove back and dropped her off at her cottage, and only then did she realise the time. It was half past six. Robert would understand, she thought, when he knew she was only late due to a mission of mercy. He was sitting there, patiently at the table, waiting for his dinner. Anne told him what had happened and why she was late as she moved about the kitchen fixing his dinner.

She managed his meal inside forty-five minutes without him saying a word, just sitting there, waiting. Placing the plate in front of him, she sat down with hers opposite him. His eyes were hard as he looked at her across the table, and then, instead of picking up his knife and fork, he picked up the plate. He stood up and then strode over to the waste bin, threw his dinner, plate as well, into the container, and still not saying a word, left the house and went to the pub up the road.

He never said a word to her for a whole month. He sat down for his breakfast at seven forty-five every morning, weekdays that was, and would leave a note by the side of his plate before leaving the table. This would only be instructions as to what he wanted for dinner that evening. Sex was withheld for three months, though this was not a hardship. They would only have nervous fumblings under the sheets once a month at the best of times. She would lie there for many a long hour after these few brief minutes and wondered if this was what love was supposed to mean.

This past reverie was brought to a halt for her to then race up the stairs to the main line station to catch the train for Bishop's Stortford. She was just in time and with help from a porter, managed to get into a carriage as he shut the door behind her.

Out of breath but still with her bags, she fell into a seat to catch her breath. She didn't travel that often into London by train, and on the journey there, she had been glued to the window for the whole short journey. Watching the fields flow past like undulating green seas, she was mesmerized by the continuous up and down motion of the telephone lines interspersed by the poles that held them up. The clickety clack of the train speeding its way to London, then slowing down so that she could see the narrow gardens of the tenements that backed onto the railway line.

But on this return journey she saw nothing but her own reflection on the window. The falling darkness, with the carriage light shining from above, showed her face almost as clearly as a mirror. It shimmered for a moment, and she saw herself as she was twelve years ago, for it was that amount of time since she got married. How proud she had felt walking down the aisle in her wedding gown, and there, waiting for her before the altar, was Robert. She had started working in the same bank as him when she was sixteen and being a naïve young girl had fallen for the man who had taken her under his wing to teach her the workings of the bank. He was six years older than she was, but that didn't matter because she was in love.

They'd honeymooned in Brighton where he took away her virginity as she had been brought up that it was only right for her husband to be the first to change her from girl to a woman. But the romance novels told of transportation to heights of rapture, to feel as though one could reach out and touch the very stars in the sky. To come alive as with the breaking of the dawn and the rising of the sun. To be covered in that warm glow as it rose, (she never did catch the analogy), and filled with its heat. But truth is not stranger than fiction. Truth is reality, and it is not found in fiction.

He had taken her virginity, but left nothing behind but his seed that never took root. He rolled off and had promptly fallen asleep, leaving her with a sense of longing. Of what, she did not know. Just that she was missing something apart from frustration. Over the years she tried to find this missing feeling, but never found it.

He was made head clerk not long after their marriage and three years later was made Assistant Manager at the branch where he now worked. There were no other vacancies in the same bank, so it was decided that his wages were now enough for them to be able to take out a mortgage. They found the cottage they now lived in, which she was beginning to realize, has since become nothing but a gilded cage. With him having the exalted title of the Assistant Manager, he became very punctilious in all that he did. Everything he did was regulated by the clock, even when they took their holidays in Brighton every year, meals, bedtime, etc.

She jumped up startled, as the train jerked its way to a stop at her station. The bus was on time for its usual run round to the villages and she knew that she had three quarters of an hour before Robert came home. Deposited at the stop by the pub, she hurried the few minutes it took to reach her cottage. With bags thrown to one side, they could be dealt with later, she rushed to the kitchen and started to prepare his dinner.

It was only after he had finished his hot chocolate drink that night in bed, given her a peck on the cheek and fallen asleep, did she give thought to the meeting in the café of the department store with the other three women. She thought of this for many nights, and it wasn't until his monthly ritual of obliging her with his sexual favours that she made her decision.

It wasn't taken lightly, because she had been thinking of nothing else since that meeting. But lying there in the dark, her body crying out for a release she didn't know how to bring about and then not quite sure what it was or what it would feel like, she thought maybe she would have a chance later.

***

JANE LEFT the cafeteria with her purchases and unlike Anne, took her time to wend her way through the people milling about, still trying to find their own particular bargain. It was only when she reached the outside did she quicken her step because of the cold wind and was grateful to feel that warm gush of air as she reached the steps to the underground. The main line station was awash with people milling around the departure boards high above their heads, babbling amongst themselves about the cancelled trains.

Without hesitation, Jane wheeled round and made for the exit and joined the queue for a taxi. It was not a long wait for they were coming in, taking passengers aboard and then whisking out of the station yard. So she was soon in the back seat of her black cab being taken to Bagshot.

'Ave ter pay extra luv, it being that far out,' he said in his cabby jargon.

'No problem, no lip, shut up and drive,' she said in as broad a cockney accent as she could.

'Well I never,' he replied, but slid the little glass window shut and did as he was told.

The journey took just on two hours, but worth it, Jane thought. It had given her time to sit back and relive that half an hour at the table. Would they or wouldn't they…

Living with a bookmaker for the past ten years had given her a good insight into the way people gamble and how to calculate the odds in nearly all situations. Now this was a new one for her, and she sat and hugged herself in trying now to assess each of the women and take bets with herself at which way they would jump. But first, she had to concentrate on herself. Off the cuff, she wondered, silently, what are the odds on you going through with the idea?

For the first time in her life, the answer didn't pop up as it would with most questions that had been thrown at her in the past. Michael, her 'Pound for a Pound' husband would make a joke that his wife could give odds that were ninety-nine times right out of a hundred, and he did listen when she made these predictions. The only times he didn't listen was when she spoke about his taking up with tarts when she wasn't around.

So she settled herself back into the softness of the taxi and reviewed herself so that she could come up with the answer to her own question. She'd been round the block more than once before she first met Michael Pound, the local bookmaker, well not really a bookmaker then. It was a few years before it was legal off course, but he took bets in the pub and took their money and paid out the winners, expecting, and getting a drink from, the winnings.

He was flashy in those pubs, not only in his clothes, but also with his friends, and taking a fancy to Jane, swept her into his circle. It didn't take long for him to get inside her pants and she enjoyed it. Not so much the sex side of it, but the constant excitement that horse racing engendered not only in the punters but in herself as she watched him take the money in, shouting for the horse the mugs backed, but secretly waiting for it to fall. He would commiserate with the losers and then slap a winner on the back and ask for a drink to celebrate his win. Two drinks, one of them being for Jane.

Working in the Greasy Spoon café didn't produce many tips, so seeing this much money keep passing through his hands was like a magnet to a lump of iron. She hung like a limpet and coaxed him to make their association legal. He eventually agreed, after being denied what he wanted, and was used to getting on a regular basis.

That was ten years ago. Now he could have what he wanted, whenever he wanted, but also took what he could get outside of the marital home; and there wasn't a shortage of that either. But then came the worry! What if he picked up something from those sluts, then came home to her!

She shuddered at the thought and had made him wear a condom ever since. This had annoyed him greatly, shouting at her that he was a bareback rider and always would be. That was the beginning of the rift between them that had slowly grown to a chasm that was getting more difficult to cross. So she tossed the mental dice and they came up as sevens.

'I don't know Bagshot, lady. Tell me where to go,' the taxi driver broke into her thoughts.

Go to hell, was the first thought that came to mind, but she gave him the directions, and when they stopped, he told her the fare, and she gave him an extra fiver and told him to give his wife a treat. It was with shouted thanks that he drove away and left her looking at the house that was home to her and Michael. But not for long you prick, she said to herself as she went down the drive and then inside.

***

AFTER SHAKING hands, Francis and Penny left the store together and hailed a taxi and they both travelled to Knightsbridge where Penny got out and gave the taxi driver a twenty pound note and told him what station to go to. She waved as it pulled out from the curb, and turning, made her way up to the front door. Penny didn't expect Bill to be home and she wasn't disappointed. She called him Bill because it annoyed him. William, he had always insisted that he be called, but when she was upset or angry, or just wanted to rile him, she called him Bill.

It was an old Victorian building that was okay in the days of gaslight and servants, but not really practical in this modern day. The rooms were too large, not just in width and length, but in height. Chandeliers had to be used to bring the illumination down lower into the room, but, the reflected prismatic patterns made upon the ceilings compensated and actually enhanced the character in its ambience.

But it was an empty house, a lonely house, inhabited only by ghosts past and present. Penny could feel them all around her as she went through each room, surveying the contents, trying to find an elusive tangible element that would say that this was hers, hers and hers alone. But there was nothing, only pieces of outdated furniture that had been left by the last owners that were not even Victorian, but just large cumbersome monstrosities that they couldn't be bothered to carry away.

She went through to the kitchen and idly opened the fridge, but what little there was in there, didn't appeal to her at all. So she pulled a bottle of wine from the rack and uncorked it. When she poured out the first glass, she only then noticed that it was a white wine. She grimaced, but drank it all the same. She was really a red wine drinker, but the bottle was open so she sat by herself in the huge kitchen at the large scrubbed refectory table and finished the bottle. Opening another bottle, this time red, and with a fresh glass, she went upstairs to her bedroom. She called it hers, because he, her husband, wasn't there that often to share it. His usual excuse was the clinic, and that he had to stay over for the night because of a seriously ill patient.

Her patience had worn out long ago and she was delighted to have met some women who had similar feelings towards their own husbands. She went through to the bathroom, and even this was too big. When the house had been built, they didn't put in such things as bathrooms or toilets. This was just another room that had been converted, and plumbing installed in the early twenties. The bath was big, enamelled cast iron on four claw-like feet with large taps and shower attachment. The water system was good though, and soon she was filling it up with hot water.

Undressing in the bedroom, the clothes she had worn were thrown into the washing basket to be sorted out later, and went back into the bathroom with the wine bottle and glass. Sprinkling in some bath oils, she stepped into the bath and eased her body down into its warm embrace. With the bottle within reach, glass full, she relaxed and thought over the meeting with the other three.

Would they go for it, she mused. Jane seemed as if she was as was Francis. Anne seemed the doubtful one, scurrying off like that. Under the thumb, but maybe the worm will turn. For herself she wanted it. She'd been married to William for eleven years now and was sick and tired of nearly always being on her own. When he did come home, she could smell the perfume of another woman on his clothes. She knew that it was these women who provide the money for this house and style of living, but was it really living? Sex with him was intermittent and no children had come from these odd joinings together.

Didn't he realise that she needed sex just as much as he did? She'd had two one night stands over the last four years, but they were not enough and were unsatisfactory at that. She wanted to pick the time and place, and more importantly, the man.

The bottle was nearly empty and the water was cooling, so she washed and then dried herself, and without putting on nightclothes, got into bed. She snuggled under the covers and put a pillow to hug between her legs, and mused over what it would be like to kill a man? Would it be like sex? Sex! She fell asleep dreaming about it.

***

FRANCIS GOT to her station a little while later after dropping off Penny and caught the train for Malden. Others on the train had been doing much the same thing as her, bags from various London stores filled seats and overhead racks. Could she go through with it? She no longer loved Stephen, though they'd been married for twenty-two years and had a daughter, Sylvia, now married and living in the States.

Their sex life now was based on him watching the late night adult channel on T.V. and then wanting what he had just seen. This could be at one or two o'clock in the morning. He'd wake her up and violently enter her, then, when he was satisfied, roll off and go to sleep. Sometimes she would just lie there, feeling his semen slowly ooze out of her and stickily slide down her inner thigh and she would silently cry.

There was no love there for her. She was just a hole for him to stick his thing in whenever he felt like it, but expected her to do everything else for him. Wash his clothes, cook his food, clean the house and just open her legs when he wanted it. Not when she wanted it, the tender kiss, the soft words of love like were said for the first couple of years.

Her hand was wet and she suddenly realised that she was crying. No sounds, but just the silent rivulets of tears coursing down her cheeks. She blinked her eyes but couldn't see for the water that filled them. Groping for her handbag, she pulled out some tissues and wiped her eyes and cheeks before blowing her nose. It's come to this she thought, sitting in a train crying for the love she had lost. Well it was not too late to find another, to recapture that bliss. She was nearly forty, but her need for love still burned deep within her and she still had lots to give herself.

So she would definitely go to meet the others next month.

***

AFTER A few days mulling things over, Penny went ahead and booked a table at the wine bar for lunch for four for the day that she hoped, they would all turn up. The three and a half weeks dragged by, her stomach churning nearly every day of that time.

Then the day arrived. Butterflies were there as she entered the bar and after giving her name, was escorted to the reserved table. She ordered a glass of red wine and then sipped at it waiting and hoping that they would all come. There was still a few minutes to go to the appointed time because she had deliberately arrived early because of the table booking. People were entering and leaving all the time, and Penny looked up each time only to be disappointed.

Then her heart leapt up to her throat and pounded away as she recognised Francis coming through the door. She gave a little wave as Francis's head turned, surveying the tables, and her face lit up when she saw Penny waving to her. Penny stood up and they both brushed cheeks as a greeting and Francis took off her coat and sat down at the table.

'Ooh I am pleased that you came,' Penny said, 'I've been sitting here on tenterhooks that I would be here all on my own.' A waiter hovered at the table and Francis looked at Penny's glass and ordered the same. Penny put her hand out and touched that of Francis. 'I'm glad that you came.'

'I nearly didn't this morning. I had such butterflies in my stomach that I threw up.'

'I felt the same,' interrupted Penny, 'but you're here now.'

'Do you think the others will come?' Francis asked, looking at her wristwatch, 'It's just gone one o'clock.'

'I don't know, but somehow I knew you would, and I thought Jane... Well speak of...here she is now.'

Jane had entered the bar and seen them straight away, and was making her way to the table.

'Hello, you two. Well I won my bet.' Both had stood up and there was the brushing of cheeks again, and Jane made herself comfortable at the table. 'White, no. Make it a large gin and tonic please,' she said to the waiter.

'What bet?' queried Francis.

'I made a bet with myself that you two would here when I arrived. So where's Anne?'

'Well not here, obviously. I had some doubts about her anyway, but, let's wait a little while, she may have been held up,' Penny said.

'I had my doubts too,' Francis chipped in, 'but not now. She's just come in.' They all turned to the door and saw Anne smile in recognition.

'I nearly didn't come,' she said breathlessly as she sat down.

'Me too,' said Francis.

'I lost that bet,' Jane said.

'I'm very glad that you did,' said Penny, patting Anne's hand. 'What do you want to drink?' She gave her order to the waiter and then they all accepted the menus from another to study what the establishment had to offer. They placed their orders and handed back the menus.

'I suggest we eat first and talk afterwards. It shouldn't take long because there's not a lot that we can discuss in such a public place,' Jane said. The others nodded their agreement and then asked each other about their journey into town and the like till lunch was served.

With lunch over and all had coffee before them, Jane spoke.

'We all know why we're here and it's basically to say yes to what was mentioned last month. I take it that we are in agreement? Francis?'

'Yes.'

'Penny?'

'Definitely,'

'Anne?'

'Yes, please.' They all laughed at this reply.

'This is like that Hitchcock film, you know, "Strangers on a Train,"' Penny said.

'And they didn't get away with it,' Anne said gloomily.

'And why?' put in Jane.

'The young one backed out from doing it,' Francis said.

'That's because he was on his own is why he couldn't go through with it,' Jane stated, 'but we will be three. That's the difference. Each backs the other two up. But we're jumping the gun here. Let's see if it's feasible when we draw up a plan. The first thing we have to do is meet again with as much detail about you know who. Photos, home, work place, drinking habits, leisure pursuits and any other small detail that you think may be of help in the planning. All clear on that?'

With nods and yes's, Jane continued. 'Shall we say next month then? Is that enough time?' Again the answer was in the affirmative.

'Where, if we can't talk here?' Anne asked.

'My place?' Penny suggested. 'Seeing as I live here it would be better. I can lay on a snack lunch and some drinks and we'll be able to say everything then. Any problems there?' No was the collective answer.

'Here's my address,' Penny wrote it down on a napkin and it was passed round the other three.

'Don't write it down,' Jane said. 'Just remember it. When you write your notes, keep one copy to bring and make sure you destroy any others that you might have made. Now the date; same as today next month?'

Agreement all round.

'Time. I suggest between ten and eleven in the morning, or shall we say not any later than eleven? Is that alright with you, Penny?' Penny nodded and again they agreed.

'So that's about as far as we can go at this stage. I say again, thanks for coming and I'll look forward to seeing you at Penny's house this time next month. Shall we say the meeting is closed? Or are there any questions?'

There weren't, so calling over the waiter, each settled their own checks, and then, with goodbyes being said, they all took their leave.

As each journeyed home, they cast their minds back over the lunch-time talk, and gave thought to what they should write down about their husbands.

***

PENNY WAS surprised that it was Anne who arrived first, exactly on the dot of ten, expecting it to be Jane.

'Come in Anne, come in,' she said in welcome, and they kissed on the cheek. 'You're the first. Here, let me take your coat.' She helped her off with it and hung it on the stand behind the front door.

'This way,' she said, leading her into the large sitting room then stopping. 'No. I think we would be a bit more comfortable in the kitchen. At least I won't have to keep traipsing back and forwards with the tea and coffee,' she rattled on, leading Anne down through the house to the kitchen. 'Now sit where you want. I'll put the kettle on.' Anne sat down, looking round the large kitchen.

'My, it's big isn't it.'

'Too bloody big for me. Nearly all the other houses are subdivided into flats. I believe that they are at least six to each house, but he wanted it for the address. Knightsbridge and all that. Bloody snob. I see you've brought some things with you. Are they, er, what we talked about?'

'Yes. I hope I've got it right,' she answered, reaching into the small carrier bag.

'Let's wait until the others come, shall we? Here's your tea and I'll just go and get my notes.' She left Anne alone in the kitchen.

The doorbell rang and Anne got up and went to the kitchen door and looked out. No sound of Penny and the bell rang again, so Anne went through the hall and opened the front door.

'Hello Anne,' Jane said in surprise. 'I've just lost my bet. With a house this size, I expected a maid to answer the door.' Anne stood aside to let her in.

'Hello Jane, nice to see you again.' They brushed cheeks just as Penny came down the stairs. 'Oh good. I was right at the top when I heard the bell. How are you, Jane?' she said, moving forward for the friendly clasp and kiss on the cheek.

'Bloody marvelous, and you?'

'Feeling much better for seeing that there's two of you here. Only Francis to come now. Let me have your coat.' She was just hanging it up when the bell sounded again and the open door revealed Francis herself.

'Just saying that you were the last.'

Hellos were said as Francis took off her coat and for Penny to hang it up for her. 'Into the kitchen with you now. Anne, show them the way, there's a dear.' When Penny finished with Francis's coat, she followed them.

'Nice big kitchen you've got here,' Jane said.

'That's what I said,' Anne answered.

Penny threw her folder on the table and put the kettle on again.

'Tea? Coffee?' It was tea for Francis and coffee for Jane. They settled at the table making small talk until the cups were put down and then Penny sat down with her cup and looked at the others.

'Well here we are. Our little circle,' Jane said.

'Hmmph. More like a square the way we're sitting, one opposite each other,' said Penny.

'The square circle,' Anne said, 'I like that.'

'That sounds good,' said Francis.

'Excellent! That's what we should use when we have to talk in public in reference to ourselves. The Square Circle, very good Anne. Now to business! Let's reaffirm why we are here.' Jane put her hand out on the table, open and with the palm upwards.

'I am here to plan and ask you three women to kill my husband. I swear not to tell another living soul of anything we say or do in respect of this matter, and here is my hand on it.'

Penny put her hand out and covered that of Jane's.

'I too am here for you three women to kill my husband. I will help and plan it and swear not to speak of this to any living soul so help me God.' Jane's hand squeezed that of Penny's. Francis placed her hand on that of the other two on the table.

'I am here for you three women to kill my husband and I will help and plan it. I swear not to speak of this to anyone at all, so help me God.'

Anne's hand slowly reached out across the table and put it, trembling slightly, with the others.

'I…I also am here to help plan for you three to kill my husband. Nothing said between us will ever pass my lips, so help me God.'

All four hands were shaken across the table, Anne's face was very white, and Penny gave her hand an extra little squeeze as she smiled at her.

'Now for us to do this right and make each one appear to be an accident, we must have meticulous planning the whole way through. So let each of us give out as much as we can about our husbands so that plans can be made for, well we know what result we want. Okay, who's going to speak first?' Jane asked.

'I'll start the ball rolling with my albatross,' Penny said.

'Pardon?' asked Jane, looking perplexed.

'Albatross,' answered Anne, 'from The Ancient Mariner,' which did nothing to enlighten her.

'William Swithers', Penny started, handing round photos, 'is thirty-nine years of age, and lives, ha, ha, at this address. His clinic is at,' she consulted her notes and told them the address, 'which is just off Sloane Square where he is a consultant.

'What exactly it is he is consulted about, I've never asked, except that I know he helps young girls who get into trouble out of the trouble they found themselves in. They're usually rich young things that the trouble would hurt their social standing as well as embarrass their parents. In other words, he gets them in the family way and then makes the parents pay a hefty fee for him to get them out of their problem. Abortionist is the word that springs to mind. We holiday on the Riviera, where he can get more girls into trouble.

'He's a non-smoker but does like to drink in a fashionable little club just off the King's Road. He's a sucker for pretty women and I'm afraid that he'd have to be lured by sex.'

'He looks a dish. I wouldn't mind being the lure if that's okay with you, Penny?' Francis said, holding his photograph in her hand.

'It would mean having sex with him, I mean. To hook him as it were.'

'That I wouldn't mind,' Francis replied with a smile.

'Well he's good in that department, if my memory serves me right,' she said, scratching her head and giving a quizzical look.

This drew small titters from them all. 'He also has a habit of trying to put people down. For example, at any function he would introduce himself and then say as an afterthought, "Oh, P.S. This is my wife Penny Swithers, get it? P.S.?" then he would laugh thinking it uproarious.' Penny gave them a weak smile.

'Well to finish it off, oh that's good! No, the last bit is that I could be taking a short vacation with friends in Paris when the deed is being done? Now that's my lot of notes, now who'll speak next?' Anne raised her hand.

'I'd like to get mine said next, please.'

'Go ahead then,' Jane replied. Anne cleared her throat and read from her notes.

'We...no...er, I....er, let me start again. His name is Robert Seymour and he is thirty-six. Our home is a cottage in Hertfordshire, about twenty-five minutes from Bishop's Stortford where he is an Assistant Bank Manager. He doesn't smoke and we don't have a car. He travels to work by bus, which he gets outside the pub, which is also the bus stop. His hobby…'

'What time?' Francis interrupted. 'The bus time, I mean.'

'At eighty twenty every morning. It drops him right outside the bank at five to nine.' Francis nodded, and Anne continued, 'His hobby is calligraphy and…'

'What's that?' queried Jane.

'Calligraphy is the art of writing. You know, fancy letters of the alphabet, like what you see in old manuscripts. He's a light drinker and only goes to the pub on a Thursday night. He leaves the house at seven thirty and from the pub at ten thirty. It takes exactly ten minutes to walk. He's a time freak, if you know what I mean. The alarm goes off at seven ten each morning. He gets up and shaves, farts and shits, if you'll excuse me,' she said, going red. 'Yes, he even shits by the clock.

Then he has a bath and is downstairs dressed and ready for his breakfast, which must be ready on the table by exactly seven forty-five. It takes him just under twenty minutes and then he's off to catch the bus. He arrives home at exactly six thirty-five, washes and changes and is at the table for his dinner at six fifty. The evenings vary slightly, except Thursday. He has hot chocolate at ten forty-five and he is asleep at eleven. There's not much variation at the weekends except he stays at home.' Anne put her notes down and looked around the table. Penny was looking at his photo.

'I'd have killed the shit years ago, you poor girl.' She put her hand out and held that of Anne.

'Yes, well that will be sorted out. Next? Francis?' Jane asked.

'Mine is called Stephen. There are several different pictures of him there. He's forty-two years old and is a civil servant. We've been married for twenty-two years now.'

'Wow,' Jane breathed, 'Oh sorry, Francis.' Francis smiled and continued.

'We have a detached house in Malden, and he drives into Chelmsford every day, parks up, and then goes on by train to London. He leaves the house at seven each morning and generally arrives home about six thirty, except on Fridays. He leaves work early so he can reach home at any time on that day. I'm not sure exactly where his office is, I just know that it's somewhere just off Whitehall. He's a moderate smoker, well they can't smoke in his building, and he doesn't drink much. We take our holidays either in Spain or Italy once a year but not always the same date.

'We have one daughter, Silvia, and she is married and lives in the States. We don't correspond that often and I think that I would like to go over there to see her when, when…. Oh hobbies, I nearly forgot. There's only one and that is watching dirty videos, you know, those late night adult channel films. That's it.'

'Well done, Francis. That leaves you, Jane. Ready?' Penny asked.

'Yes. Michael Pound. Self-made bookmaker. Started by taking bets on street corners and pubs till it was made legal. We live in a big house outside Bagshot. We have a car, but he also uses cabs. No children. No hobbies except reading anything about racing. I don't go to every meeting and I know that when I don't, he picks up some tart and then I might not see him for several days. Heavy smoker and drinks a lot. He only goes to the North of England when it's a really big race meeting, otherwise he confines himself to the Southern courses. We go to Spain most times for a holiday when the flat season ends, that's if he's made enough money. If it's alright with you all, I'd like to take a cruise when it's my turn.' She smiled at this last remark. 'Thank you all, I think we've done very well.'

'Yes,' Penny said, 'now it's time for lunch, who's going to help?' They all helped in one way or another, getting plates out, prepared dishes from the fridge. Glasses were found as Penny opened some wine bottles. It was a merry little lunch for them all, happy they had now made the first steps towards their own personal freedom.

They washed and dried up the dishes and with their glasses re-filled, took their places back at the table.

'Before we can even think of our plans for, for what we are, sorry, for what we *will* do,' said Jane, 'we must first get them to sign the necessary forms increasing their life insurance. This is going to be the hardest task of all. Each of us has got to convince the men that more insurance cover is needed. Also it is going to take time, so don't get agitated, and carry on as normal. Because we won't be able to control how much they are going to be insured for, we'll have to set up some means of pooling the money so that we can have an equal share out when it's all over.

'We'll come back to that later. I've given it a lot of thought and we have to be able to communicate with each other without revealing our identity to any outsiders or any investigation.'

Jane paused and took a sip of her wine.

'Let's use it alphabetical so that we all will know who is being referred to. Anne being number one so Francis will be number two, then me as three and Penny as four. This will not be the necessary order for what will come later. I'm sorry to be doing all the talking, please jump in at any time if you want to,' Jane said.

'You're doing just fine, Jane,' Penny said going to the wine rack and getting, and opening another bottle. The other two nodded, glad that one of the others had taken up the baton so to speak.

'Okay. Now let's start the insurance ball rolling? First is that we've got to come up with some story for our husbands. You've got to convince him that you both need it. Like if you have a mortgage, that's got to be paid off. Funeral expenses are going up. Oh what will I do without you to look after me, wailing with a wringing of hands? You get the idea?' They all nodded. 'Get him to go for as much as the insurance company will swallow bearing in mind his age. Then, when all is signed and sealed, let us know. First the name of the insurance company.......' Penny interrupted her.

'Shouldn't we know now what insurance companies we use? This will save time.'

'Quite right,' Jane conceded and they all in turn said what company they were already using. With both Jane and Penny using the same one, Jane said that she would seek out another one to use.

'Phew, this is thirsty work,' she said and took several large sips from her glass and Penny refilled it for her.

'Now how to communicate privately,' she said continuing. 'Each of us should use some Internet café, not the nearest one, and set up an E-mail address as soon as possible using your own personal number in the address, but let us avoid using the square circle in this. Then we can meet again and pass them across to each other, but try to remember them, because any copies must be destroyed when we actually begin operations.

'With these addresses set up we only need to check them sporadically till the insurance side is tied up. Now any questions?'

'Yes,' from Penny. 'How long do you think that would be?'

'Let's hope it's not longer than a couple of months.'

'And the other bit, you know?' Anne asked.

'To sort out all four, we'll see if we can do it within four months.'

'That'll be about six months then,' Anne again.

'Oh shit. I would like mine to be out of the way next week,' Francis said with a resigned look on her face.

'But look at the payout,' Penny chipped in.

'That I've got to look into about the money being pooled without our names being linked and yet we can still get it out when we want to share out. Now the last thing for this meeting is to say that let's actually get together sometimes where it looks like we can make the accidents happen. We need to view the locations for all sorts of reasons, so we do a survey, talk it over, make a plan and then pick holes in it. We'll have about three months to work them out, so let's not worry too much about it at the moment. If that's it then, let's meet up in four weeks' time here, just to pass out our E-mail addresses, if that's alright with you, Penny?'

'No problem,' she replied.

'Okay, all happy with that?' Jane asked.

There were murmurs of agreement and they all got up and made their way to the hall and put on their coats.

'Do we have to leave at five minute intervals and take different routes?' Anne asked. The others laughed.

'Not at this stage, I should think. Not until after the insurance side is completed,' Penny laughed. 'You've seen too many spy films.'

With that, they all kissed cheeks and the three girls said goodbye to Penny till the following month.

***

IT DIDN'T take Penny long to set up her E-mail address, and hoped that the others found it just as easy. What took her quite a bit of time was trying to gather documentation as to extent of the finances of William and herself, and then what insurance policies they had, and how much they would realise when converted. It worked out that if he were to die the next day, the insurance would not even cover the existing mortgage. She then calculated his future income for another twenty years based on what he had told her a few years ago, halved it, and that was what she wanted the new policy to pay out. Now she had to get him to agree to it.

Then she was most surprised that when she broached the subject a few days later he agreed with her. Get the insurance company to send round an agent and sort it out, he told her. The agent duly visited her and told her what the additional premium would cost, left her the filled in papers for her husband's signature and left. William signed them that evening.

This was just a few days before the square circle met again.

***

ANNE AND Francis met coming out of the tube station and had walked to Penny's house together and met up with Jane at the corner of the street. So with the door only being opened once, they were gathered together again. After the normal greetings, they were soon around the kitchen table again with their coffee and tea. Penny was bubbling inside, but held back to make it a surprise at the end.

'Francis?' Jane asked, taking the chair again.

'Yes I have my address. I've made three copies, here,' and she passed round the slips of paper.

'Oh, I didn't make copies,' said Anne.

'It doesn't matter,' said Jane, 'we can copy your one.'

'Well here's it is,' and Anne waited for them to note it down and then took it back and put it in her handbag. Jane then passed hers round and so did Penny.

'Now how are we getting on with the insurance?' Jane asked. 'Anne?'

'Well I've got to first base. Robert working in a bank helps in that he knows the value of insurance, but I don't know how much I can push him to go for.' Anne said rather apologetically.

'Well hit him with the fact that in ten, twenty years from now, the cost of living, hell everything will be more than double what it is now. That's what I'm hitting Stephen with,' Francis said.

'I've hit on a way of getting Mike to sign the goddam papers. I do his tax returns for him. All I do is get lots of papers that he has to sign and just slip the insurance one in the middle for his signature,' Jane assured them. They looked at Penny and she was smiling back at them.

'I've saved us a few months,' she said gleefully. 'William's already signed his form and I've posted it.'

'Well done!' Jane said

'Hooray,' cried Anne.

'Now we're moving somewhere,' Francis said with a laugh.

'Yes we are now on the road,' Penny agreed, and told them which insurance company and for how much.

***

EVENTS BEGAN moving faster than they had planned. They all thought that as soon as they got the insurance side tied up, they could get on with it, and E-mails began to cross each other.

'From number three to number one. Tied up, etc.'

'One to two. Not as much as four, but...etc.'

'Three to two. Please slow down.'

'Two to three. Too late. Details are....'

'Four to numbers one, two and three. Meet my place, same time, ten days from this date.'

***

IT WAS only two months since they last sat round the kitchen table at Penny's, and they looked abashed at just having received a tongue lashing from Jane.

'Two months! It should have been spread over six at least. Insurance companies do talk to each other. What would happen if four insurance agents from different companies got together for a drink, and each boasted that they'd just sold a hefty life insurance policy? Wouldn't something click? It damn well would if I were one of them!' She slammed her hand on the kitchen table and knocked back her glass of wine.

'The only good thing is,' she said after Penny had refilled her glass, 'that they are all with different companies, and spread around the country. What's done is done, it can't be helped now.'

'For pooling the money, I have an idea,' Penny said, 'but I've not yet sorted out the details. Meanwhile, I've gone through the notes you left here, and come up with some ideas, but we've actually got to go over the ground ourselves. To find the right places for what we are going to do. As I said before, some will have to be entrapped by sex. I'm prepared to do it if necessary and you offered, I believe Francis, with my William?'

'Yes please,' she smiled round at the others.

'The one I think that I'll have to take on will be Michael,' looking at Jane, 'that okay with you?'

'Can you look like a tart?' she asked.

'You don't have to look like a tart to be one, ducky,' Penny replied.

'I think I should be saying Touché to that, but somehow I feel that I would be wrong,' Jane said with a frown.

'Correct,' Penny said dryly. 'To continue. The operation involving Francis would take at least three weeks to get him on the hook. With me, one week, maybe two. So for all of us to be available, these two would be either third or fourth to be done. Now also from the notes, Anne must be freed first so that she can then be available at all times, making Stephen second to free up Francis for her role playing. Any questions so far?'

'Why mine first? Not that I'm objecting.' Anne asked.

'No offence intended, but you seem to be the one of us who is tied down the most. It seems that you would have the most difficulty in getting out on your own, and Robert has fixed habits, which help us.'

'True, so I get to go on holiday?' she said with a smile in her voice.

'Yes. But you will be the grief-stricken wife when you are told the news on your return. As we all will when our turn comes round.' Chuckles of laughter and smiles round the table.

'But how do I suddenly get to go on holiday, and where does the money come from?' Anne asked, a frown creasing her face. 'He won't give it to me just like that.'

'What you've got to do is just say that you've decided you need a break. A holiday and say that you are going whether he likes it or not. You bumped into an old school friend who said that because another friend of hers dropped out at the last moment and you were offered the chance of this free holiday. Then you can book it two weeks before we hit. You do have a passport?'

'Yes, but he'll argue against me going.'

'Let him,' said Jane, 'put your foot down. It'll only be for a short time that you've got to worry about him.'

Anne nodded and fell silent, 'I'll do it,' she said quietly.

'Can you get out Thursday, Jane, Francis?' Penny asked them. Both said that they would manage somehow. 'Okay. Be here by lunchtime on Thursday. I'll have a hire car ready and we can look over Anne's village.'

The meeting broke up and as they were going out, Penny put her arm round Anne's shoulder and pushed an envelope into her bag.

'Book the holiday as soon as possible, because I've got an idea we will be able to sort it out over the next two weeks. So three weeks from now, be off skiing in Switzerland. There's enough money there for the ticket and something to spend while you're there. No,' putting her finger up to Anne's lips, 'save it for when we meet after you get back. When you're able, check your E-mail. Now have a nice holiday because we won't see you till we call a meeting after it's done. But don't forget the grieving part when you're told the news. Just don't overdo it, that's all.' She gave her a kiss on the lips and gently eased her out to join the others.

Thursday soon came round and the three of them set off in the hired car with Penny driving. She took it easy, and it was late afternoon when they arrived at the outskirts of the village where Anne and her husband Robert lived. Penny pulled into a field gateway just before the houses started. Jane got out of the car.

'Now the cottage is called Willowbank. Count your paces from here to the cottage, note it, and the number of paces to the pub forecourt, okay?'

'Got it,' said Jane, and started to walk slowly towards the village. Penny restarted the car and moved, passing Jane as she walked.

'Keep your eyes open for the cottage,' Penny said.

'That's it!' Francis exclaimed, turning to Penny after they'd passed a few. 'Did you see it?'

'Yes.' Penny could see the pub farther up the road and about halfway from there was a cottage with a lych-gate. 'See that little thatched gate there?'

'Yes.'

'I want you to walk from the pub to that gate and see how many minutes it takes. Then carry on down to the spot where we dropped Jane and we'll pick you up there.'

'Okay, and here's the pub.' Penny drove on past and a little further on stopped the car and reversed into a gateway and slowly started back. She stopped short of the pub and let Francis out, who then carried on walking down past the pub. Penny watched as Francis glanced at her wristwatch. When the two walking girls met, they didn't stop, but kept on walking. She sat and waited, watching Jane come past the pub and then she was at the car and got into the front seat.

'Got it?'

'Yes.'

'Well write it down, here.' She handed Jane a piece of paper and a pen. 'Also, did you notice a gate with a little thatched roof over it?'

'Yes, why?'

'When I move off from here, I want to know to the exact second when we reach it. Okay, ready?' Jane was looking at her watch, pausing.

'Now!'

Penny let in the clutch and moved off quietly, gathering speed as she passed the pub, reaching sixty five miles an hour as she passed the designated gate.

'Now,' she shouted as they flew past the gate and Francis, quickly slowing down to thirty and then pulling into the field gateway.

'Seven and half, maybe eight seconds,' Jane said.

'Note that down as well, and when Francis gets in, note down what she's timed.'

Francis reached the car and climbed into the back seat and leaned back with a sigh. She related the paces and the time, which Jane noted down.

'What now?' Jane asked.

'That's enough. I thought we would have to stay here till this evening, but I think the plan I've devised will work. So we'll head off back home and I can do another run on my own next week, just to confirm it.'

They talked on the return journey, but Penny asked that they leave her out of the conversation because she wanted to think, and to plan. It was early evening when they arrived and Penny asked if they could stay but a half hour and listen to her. They agreed and went inside where she poured them wine and sat them down at the kitchen table to listen.

Jane and Francis listened in rapt silence as Penny went over her plan and when she had finished, they wholeheartedly agreed with it. Penny just wanted the next Thursday night to see if it was feasible, and if so, they would kill Robert Seymour in two weeks' time.

Penny checked her E-mail before the last reconnoitre and read that Anne was off to Switzerland on Saturday and would be away for a week. Then she did a dry run that night and was satisfied that the plan would work. E-mails went out to numbers two and three to meet at the usual place on the Thursday by two p.m., wearing dark clothing.

***

FRANCIS AND Jane arrived at the house just five minutes apart, Francis on foot and Jane by car. Francis had a glass of wine but Penny and Jane abstained, as they would be driving. Laid out on the table was a pencil drawing of the village street showing the pub, the lych-gate, the cottage and the field gate. They went over the plan again and the positions and the timings. When she was satisfied that they all knew their roles, Penny burnt the plan and all of Anne's notes including the photos, which had been studied for the last time.

Jane drove her own car with Francis and Penny in the back, their destination, Euston station. The parking spot was some distance from the station, and using the pay machine, to be valid for the time they needed.

They made their way to the main line station and went into the ladies toilets. They had to wait a few minutes before they could occupy two stalls with one between them. Penny entered one and Jane, the other. Francis waited, using one of the mirrors to apply her make-up, waiting for this stall to be occupied by their victim. The stall was used twice before a young woman that Francis thought might be okay, went in and shut the cubicle door. At this, Francis then tapped once on Penny's and once on Jane's door. This was their signal to quickly glance under the lower edge and into the cubicle between them, to see which side the woman had put down her handbag.

The woman in the middle had put it down on the side by Jane's cubicle. With her just settling herself down on the seat, a hand came wiggling out from under the partition on Penny's side.

'I'm out of paper, can you help please?'

With the hand waving about, the woman did the natural thing, knowing the problem. She pulled several sheets off the roll in her cubicle and leaned forward and put them in the waiting hand.

'Thanks,' was the reply as the hand disappeared, but her handbag disappeared at the same time from the opposite side. The doors of Penny's and Jane's opened quietly and with toilets unflushed, quickly left with Francis. It was three minutes later that the woman realised her bag had gone, and another six minutes before finding a station official to report the theft. The three girls had just reached Jane's car in this period of time. Inside, the bag was passed to Jane who was wearing gloves, opened it and withdrew the woman's wallet.

'Shit!' was the exclamation from Jane. 'No fucking license!'

Plan B was King's Cross station. The handbag was tossed out on the way, and the wallet separately.

It was exactly the same procedure there, and they found a driving license in the handbag they had filched. So the first stage had been completed. Second stage was that they then drove down to Victoria Bus station, the handbag and wallet, minus cards were disposed of on the way. Here, they parked up and went off for tea as they still had some time to kill. It was nearly seven o'clock before Penny presented herself at the Avis car rental desk.

She had practised for a little while on the signature of the stolen driving license. She was smartly dressed, wearing a black wig and plain glasses and asked to hire a large Mercedes with the proviso that it could be left at Heathrow before she flew out. No problems there. She signed the forms with the name on the presented driving license and paid in cash, which came from the same wallet as the license.

She flashed her headlights as she passed the parked car of Jane, who then pulled out and followed the black Mercedes out from West London and onto the M4. They were still ahead of time, so they stopped in a motorway service station and had coffee, at different tables. With the time approaching, Penny gave a signal, and they got up and returned to their cars. Jane followed Penny and all the way to Anne's village. Slowing down as the time ticked on, Penny stopped just past the field gate, allowing Jane to pull in. A few whispered words and then Penny moved off and reached the pub car park and reversed the car so that she was then facing back down the road and yet could still see the pub's entrance. There she waited.

Francis and Jane checked their watches and at a quarter past ten, got out of the car and started walking slowly up the street towards the pub. They stopped at Willowbank cottage and Francis patted Jane on the shoulder for her to move off to the halfway point, that being the cottage with the thatched gate.

The road was dark but she could just see the lights from the pub spilling out into the night. She stopped at this gate dead on ten thirty, then watched and waited for the signal.

Penny waited, watching the pub, her eyes flicking back and forth between the car clock and the door. Then on the dot of ten thirty, the door opened, and Anne's husband emerged. The women had two signals: one for if he was alone and another for if other people were present.

He was alone. He came down the steps and Penny could see that it was the man from Anne's photographs. As he stepped off the gravel and onto the road, Penny turned off her lights for two seconds and then turned them back on before turning them off again.

Both Francis and Jane saw the signal from Penny that said go, and went into action. Jane lay down on the roadside and Francis crouched down so that she would be able to see the back lit figure of Robert walking down the road. Jane watched him approach, heart was thumping like crazy inside her chest and she could feel sweat starting to spring out on her forehead as he came closer and closer. Then it was her cue to act.

'Help me please,' she wailed. He hurried the last few paces and stopped. 'Oh thank God. Help me up please, I've hurt my ankle.' She raised her arm for him to grasp. He helped her up from the road. 'Thank you, thank you. I was just coming to see my sister when I slipped. Oh there she is.' Robert turned and saw a torch weaving its way along the roadside. This torch was also the signal for Penny.

As Francis reached Jane and Robert, Penny had slipped the car into first gear and silently glided past the pub picking up speed as it did so. Jane was hanging onto Robert's arm and Francis stopped beside her, her back to the hedge, Robert in front of her. She could see the car coming down, gathering speed every foot of the way until it was just about ten yards away.

'Now!' came from Francis and, with Jane who had straightened up, violently pushed Robert out into the path of the black Mercedes.

At sixty-seven miles an hour, the bonnet of the car struck him, breaking nearly every bone between head and ankles with a heavy crunch. The force of the car threw him high into the air, to bounce three times before rolling into the ditch alongside the road, nearly thirty feet away from the point of impact.

The car did not slow or stop, and Penny didn't turn the lights on till she had passed Jane's car parked up at the gate. Then she slowed down and went at a reasonable pace till the lights of Jane's car showed up in her mirror.

When she had seen Robert leave the pub, alone, her pulse rate increased and her heart started to beat very fast in her chest. Then she saw the torch wave and she put her foot down. The car quickly built up speed, passing the pub and going faster and faster till he suddenly loomed up in the dark.

The sudden check of the forward motion of the car as she hit the solid body of the man that disappeared as fast as it had come out of the dark. She had an orgasm, thrilled at the knowledge that she had just killed a man. The heat flowed from her chest and through her stomach and was an intense wave deep in her lower belly, and she felt her fluids seep out between her thighs as she swept past Jane's car.

Jane had a similar thrill as she saw Robert soar through the air to land with a thump further down the road and disappear into the darkness. Hand in hand with Francis, they ran down to where he'd disappeared and stopped when they found him half in and half out of the ditch. Francis bent down and felt around his neck, but couldn't feel a pulse. Jane rolled him the rest of the way into the ditch so that he was face down in the shallow water that had collected there.

Then, very quickly, they walked on down to the car. Without turning on the lights, Jane turned the car round and was soon off after Penny. At the first bend, she turned her lights on and then raced on to catch up with Penny. They caught up and then cruised behind, only dropping back as they approached the M4.

They drove on to Heathrow Airport where Penny parked the car amongst others by the Avis office. She left the keys in the ignition and walked to the end of parking lot and was then picked up by Jane.

'By God we did it,' Penny said breathlessly as she heaved herself into the back seat, and hanging onto the forward head rests, kissed Francis on one cheek and Jane on the other.

'It made me jump,' declared Francis, 'one minute he was there in the road, next, gone.'

'It nearly made me wet myself,' Jane said, concentrating on getting out into the correct lane on the M4.

'I did wet myself,' laughed Penny, 'but it wasn't pee.'

'You didn't?' screamed Jane, also laughing.

'Want to feel?' Penny choked out from her laughing.

'Not while I'm driving,' Jane managed to say, having to avoid a speeding car.

'I need a bloody good drink,' Francis declared.

'So do I,' Jane said, 'my throat's so dry.'

'Me as well, but let's get off the motorway first,' Penny said.

'Pubs will be shut by then,' Jane said.

'What time is your last train?' Penny asked Francis.

'Well if we can go straight on through,' she said, looking at her watch, 'I should be in time for the train, but no time for a drink. Let me get the train. We can have that drink another day.'

'So be it. That alright with you, Jane?' Penny asked.

'No problem.'

So they carried on the M4 and through to the station for Francis to get her train home. Penny moved into the front passenger seat and gave Francis a kiss on the cheek. 'We did well tonight. Keep an eye out for the E-mails, goodnight.'

Francis waved as they drove away and she made her way into the station. Jane and Penny drove in silence, threading through the nighttime traffic to Knightsbridge, eventually pulling up outside Penny's house.

'Come in for a drink. I think we both need one.'

Jane locked the car, put some money in the meter and followed Penny into the house. They gravitated to the kitchen and both had large gins with only a little tonic in each glass. They soon had a second one, with which they sat down and started to relax.

'Where is your er, William?' Jane asked. Penny looked at her watch.

'Well as it's after twelve, he won't be coming home tonight.'

'After twelve? Shit. I've still got to drive down to Bagshot.'

'Well you don't have to. You can stay here for the night if you want to.'

'It would beat trying to drive, tired as I am after these two drinks. Fine! I'll stay, thanks.'

'Then let's have another drink.'

They sat drinking till two a.m. going over the whole thing again to see if they had made any mistakes. Then seeing what the time was, Penny suggested that it was time for bed. They went upstairs, arm in arm.

'Do you know I had an orgasm when I hit him,' Penny confided in Jane as they went. 'Never experienced anything like that before.'

'Never?'

'No.'

'I nearly did too when he suddenly disappeared,' said Jane.

'Well here's your room,' Penny stopped outside a closed door, still holding Jane's arm in hers. 'That is...that is...if,' Penny's voice faltered.

'Would you like me to come into your bed?' Jane said softly, looking into Penny's eyes.

'Er, yes, if you would like to,' Penny stammered.

'Maybe I'll get that orgasm I missed earlier,' Jane whispered as she hugged Penny's arm tighter.

Jane had her orgasm along with Penny, and they lay in each other's arms till morning.

***

FIVE LINES in the stop press late extra of The Evening Standard on Friday evening. Nothing in Saturday's papers and only a short fill-in item in one of the Sunday papers.

Hit and Run. Local Hertfordshire village man victim of a hit and run accident. Car not traced.

The three women were on tenterhooks over the weekend but couldn't do anything about it. It was a case of just sweating it out until they had word from Anne, and she wasn't due back till Saturday.

The daily papers were scanned, but nothing else was reported.

***

ANNE LANDED at Heathrow just after lunch on the Saturday. She was tanned from the snow glare and carrying an extra bag that contained her duty free items, including a present for her husband she had the foresight to purchase. She got a bus to Bishop's Stortford and then a taxi for the short run to her cottage. A police car was parked outside, and the taxi pulled over behind it. She got out and the driver brought her case round from the trunk. She paid him, opened the gate and walked up the path. Her heart had started thumping as soon as she'd seen the patrol vehicle. It was now pounding with every step she made toward her front door.

'Excuse me,' a woman's voice came to her from behind. She stopped dead, but didn't turn round till the voice spoke again.

'Excuse me, but are you Mrs. Seymour?'

Anne slowly turned to see a policewoman standing on the path.

'Yes. I am.'

'Can we go inside and talk, please?' The woman's hand extended towards the door. Anne turned and, putting her case and bag down, got her keys out of her handbag and opened the door. She picked her bags up and went into the sitting room with the young policewoman following her, closing the cottage door behind. She put the bags back down and faced her.

'Would you like to sit down, please.'

'Why?'

'I'm afraid I've got some bad news for you.' Anne slowly backed away and sat down, eyes wide as she stared at the woman.

'It's your husband. He's had an accident and I'm afraid he's dead.'

Anne dropped her face into her hands and sobbed.

'Oh my God.' Forcing pictures into her mind, she managed to produce real tears. They came and she let them flow down her cheeks before raising her head.

'We only talked of something like this just a few months ago. What happened? Was there a bank raid?' The tears now ran freely.

'No,' the young woman said sympathetically, 'he was knocked down by a car just outside on Thursday night.' Anne had guessed while in Switzerland, that it would be done on the Thursday, so she had gotten rather drunk that evening.

'And there I was enjoying myself,' in her mind was a picture of the young ski instructor lying on top of her, his rampant sex bringing her to two orgasms before he came with a tremendous burst inside her, 'Ski-ing,' she finished with more sobs.

'Would you like me to make you a cup of tea?'

Anne nodded, fumbling with her bag for some tissues. When the policewoman came back into the room with the cup and saucer, Anne was sitting there with a little package in her hand. She took the tea and held up the package.

'I bought a little present for him too,' letting the tears run again.

'Drink the tea,' the woman said softly, 'it will do you good.'

Anne wiped her face again and dutifully drank the tea.

'Now you've had a very bad shock, but it's best to get it all done at once. I'm afraid that you will have to come with me for a positive identification. It's something that has to be done by the nearest relative. It's cruel to ask you to do this, but it has to be done. Okay?' Anne nodded, and got up and went out with her to the police car.

They drove to the hospital and eventually arrived down in the morgue's viewing room. She had to wait a few minutes while the policewoman spoke to somebody outside the door, then entered and stood next to Anne at the room's only window. An attendant wheeled a covered trolley before it, and uncovered just the head of her husband.

'Is that your husband, Robert Seymour?' Anne nodded, and the woman gave a wave at the window and the attendant covered him up again. 'Thank you, Mrs. Seymour, I'll run you back home now.'

The policewoman kept talking as they drove back, a common practice to keep a conversation going so as to keep the other person calm and not dwell on what they had just seen. Also it had another purpose, and that was to find out where Anne had been that night. She answered all the questions asked. Yes, a short break skiing in Switzerland. Last Saturday till today. Talked of the lodge, the snow, the sun and the flights, and the policewoman was satisfied when she let Anne out back at the cottage. Anne thanked her for her kindness and no, she didn't want company, she'd rather be left alone.

It wasn't till the evening that it really hit home that he was gone. His clothes in the wardrobe, his shaving gear in the bathroom and his slippers by the bed. She sat down on the edge of the bed and let her feet slip into them and then she cried. She pulled the duvet cover over herself and cried herself to sleep.

The car was not found because the damaged Mercedes wasn't reported to the police. It was noted down at Avis, but assumed it had happened in the car park, so it only went through on their own insurance. They tried to contact the woman who hired it, but the driving license was out of date as the woman had moved and not notified the D.V.L.A. about a change of address.

The autopsy had been performed that gave the cause of death as the result of being struck by a moving vehicle. The inquiry confirmed that a person or persons unknown due to careless or dangerous driving had unlawfully killed Robert Seymour. The body was released and he was buried three weeks after the 'accident,' attended by Anne and some of the bank personnel.

None of the three girls attended.

During those three weeks, Jane and Penny had travelled over various routes from Chelmsford to Malden on different days and at different times, and finally decided on a location for what they had in mind.

Francis, at the last meeting, came with a good find. Somebody had used a birth certificate as a book mark and she had found it after she had bought a second hand book off a market stall. This she handed over and also lent Penny a black wig she had bought some time ago.

Now wearing this wig and a pair of plain glasses and armed with the birth certificate, she visited various letting agents and viewed properties close to William's favourite watering hole off the King's Road, Chelsea. She settled on one just round the corner and less than two minutes from the club. The rent was exorbitant, but she didn't argue and took it for six months, paying in cash, using the birth certificate as proof of identity.

Jane went and hovered around Bagshot to pick up the local papers to follow the progress of Anne's defunct husband, so noted the funeral date.

An E-mail was sent to Francis. *From three to two. Prepare for visit to States in three or four weeks time. Advise when departure date fixed.*

Her heart leaped into her throat when Francis read this in the café. She wiped the message and went straight to the pub and had a stiff drink. In fact, she had two while sorting out what she had to do. First to phone her daughter to tell her of the impending visit, then to find out the plane schedules. Only after the flight had been booked would she tell her husband of her trip.

E-mails went out to numbers one and four to meet at the usual place, giving date and time. Then a first class letter to Anne's address with just a curt note. *'Check E-mail. Destroy this note. Three.'*

Anne read this and destroyed it, and then next day went into Bishop's Stortford to read the message.

Jane told her husband, Michael, that she would be off visiting an old friend and might stay the night.

***

THEY MET at Penny's house in time for the lunch she had prepared, Jane being the first to arrive. They embraced and had what is more than a normal kiss on the greeting of each other. Their eyes looking deep into each other's as they broke apart, just as Anne arrived. She came through the door, her face pale and drawn, and as soon as Penny embraced her, she burst into tears. Jane quickly came to her side and held her as Penny did. They slowly moved down to the kitchen, supporting Anne all the way and sat her down in a chair. Penny quickly poured out a large vodka into a water glass and handed it to her. She gulped at it and as the raw spirit hit the back of her throat, she started to cough and choke. They patted her back during the coughing spell, but it had done the trick.

'I'm sorry,' she spluttered when she got her breath back, 'I didn't mean to make a scene, but….but, well I didn't know what to expect.'

She got a handkerchief out and blew her nose and then wiped her eyes. She looked up at both of them standing either side of her, holding a hand each, her eyes shining.

'Thank you. Thank you both,' she said softly.

'Well it's your turn to help Francis now,' said Jane.

'Anything. Anything at all!'

'Don't be too anxious,' said Penny, 'We've cast you in the starring role.'

'Oh, what's that?'

'Well after spending odd days over the last three weeks casing the joint, so to speak, we've come up with this.'

Penny then produced a large piece of paper that looked like a map with roads and a river marked on it. There were other markings upon it, which Penny went on to explain as she revealed the plan she and Jane had come up with. Anne clapped her hands and approved it wholeheartedly. Almost forgetting her recent loss, she was all for it - even the part where she had to take all her clothes off in front of a strange man, as if she hadn't done so in Switzerland anyway.

'Well what do you really think?' Penny asked.

'I think it will work,' said Anne.

'What if he doesn't show? He might not take that route. Don't forget that Francis is only away for two weeks,' Jane said, putting in her pennyworth.

'Then she gets an extended holiday till the job's done. So, did you bring your car?' Penny asked of Jane.

'Of course!' Jane replied.

'Shall we go for a ride then and look over the area?'

'Yes,' came from Anne and Jane.

So off they set and Jane drove them with great expertise through the traffic and emerged from North London on the road to Chelmsford.

'Now this is the station.' It was an obvious fact, but Penny had spoken up for Anne's benefit and was laying down the groundwork.

'He picks his car up from over there,' indicating the commuters' car park, 'and he goes off this way,' she said, pointing. Jane then drove off in that direction and followed Penny's advice as she had the map as to the roads to take to lead them out into the countryside and the road to the village where he lived.

'We followed him last week and this is the route he took. We just hope that he keeps to it.' She pointed out the salient points and then where they would be at the critical time. They then turned round and returned to London.

Jane asked if Anne minded being dropped off at the station, because she had other things to do before returning home herself. Penny felt the inner sides of her thighs start to tingle when she heard Jane say this. Anne said it was fine, and so she was dropped off to make her way home. But just before they reached the station, it was agreed that they go for the hit a week on Friday, and to meet at Penny's no later than nine a.m.

They were just turning into the street where Penny lived when she asked Jane. 'Did you really have other things to do on the way home?'

'No,' was the laconic reply.

The car was parked and Penny took from her bag a resident's parking permit, which Jane put on the dashboard before locking the car. It was still early evening and traffic wardens were still on the prowl. Penny opened the door to the house and they both went inside and through to the kitchen.

'Do you live in the kitchen?' Jane asked.

'Mostly. It's either here or the bedroom. Coffee, wine and food are all here, and the t.v., if I want to watch anything while I'm cooking and eating. Do you like spaghetti?'

'Yes,' said Jane, somewhat surprised at the question.

'Then you'll stay for dinner. Spaghetti Bolognese, but cooked the Spanish way.' Penny bustled round the kitchen getting out all the ingredients, and opening some wine, poured them both a large glass each. Then she got out the makings for a salad and asked if Jane would like to make it to go with the spaghetti.

It was starting to get dark but instead of turning on the light, Penny got some candles out, little ones that have different aromas when lit. These were placed around the kitchen and they cast strange shadows in the gathering gloom in that large kitchen. The Bolognese was ready, the spaghetti was ready and the salad was on the table. A platter was filled with the spaghetti and the Bolognese was poured over the top, seeping down through the thin strands of pasta, and that was then placed on the table at the end.

Penny sat at the end of the table and Jane at the seat on the side, next to her. Their glasses were filled with red wine that looked like blood in the flickering light of the candles. They lifted their glasses in a silent toast to each other and took a sip.

'Let's eat,' said Penny, picking up her fork, and they both started to tackle that huge platter between them. Napkins had to be used to wipe the dribbles of sauce as it ran down chins. Jane giggled and started to laugh.

'Sorry,' she spluttered, sending sauce in little spittle's across the table. 'I was thinking of that film, "The Lady and the Tramp." You know, where the two dogs were eating spaghetti. The same strand; and their lips met in a kiss and the she dog was so embarrassed that she blushed. Remember that?'

'I do!' Penny laughed with her, 'I wonder if we'll find the same strand.'

'I wouldn't mind if we did,' Jane said quietly. Penny blushed and went on eating.

The meal, for them was finished, though the platter still had some left. Both had given up and admitted defeat, sitting back and patting full stomachs, a slight belch emerging which caused some laughter. Jane got up and started to clear the table.

'Leave that. I'll do it in the morning,' Penny said, so Jane sat down again. Penny then stood up and stopped next to Jane. 'Can I sit on your lap for a moment?' she asked in a shaky voice. Jane moved her chair back slightly for her to do so, and Penny sat down on Jane's thighs and put her arm around her neck, her head in the hollow between shoulder and head.

'I seem to be doing most of the talking at our meetings, but I'm not as strong as it might appear. Are we doing the right thing?'

'Of course we are,' Jane assured her, stroking the hair alongside her face. 'You're the strength of the circle.'

'Am I doing this for personal reasons? Is it because the man I married does not love me enough? I don't know. All I want is some loving. Can you understand that, Jane?'

Penny's voice was muffled in the shoulder of Jane, but clearly audible to her. Also she was aware of the breast pressing against her, and she raised her other hand and gently placed it on the other breast of Penny and gently rubbed it through the material of her dress.

'I love you,' Jane said in a soft voice, slowly massaging the breast in her hand.

'Do you really?' came Penny's muffled voice, her own hand covering that of Jane's and lifting it, and slipping it inside the top of her dress so that it touched and felt the bare breast and could also feel the hard nipple.

Jane moved her shoulder so that Penny had to lift her head, and as she looked up, Jane's head bent down and kissed Penny on the lips and murmured, 'I love you, even if he doesn't.'

'You'll stay the night, won't you? Take me to bed and hold me, and, and love me?' Penny asked in a small voice.

'Of course I will,' Jane said in her soft voice, her heart exulting at how easy it had been to get what she had wanted since she'd first set eyes on her.

They made languorous love next morning when they awoke before having a shower and then breakfast together. Jane then gave Penny a loving kiss before leaving to go home. Penny, still in her bathrobe, returned it at the door, and when it closed, smiled and hugged herself at finding a new lover to replace William. So sexually excited was she at this, she actually fell to the floor of the hall and rolled herself across the cold tiles to cool down the heat that she had generated within herself.

***

AN E-MAIL from two to three gave the date and time of departure and phone contact number, and a code had been set up between Francis and Jane to be used in case of any mishaps.

With Francis leaving on a Tuesday, it was set that they would do the hit on the Friday afternoon. Jane had been dropped off to take up her position, and her car with Anne inside was parked just outside of Chelmsford on the road that Stephen Mann should take to get home.

Penny was at the station to await his arrival, based on the notes from Francis. Each of them had a mobile phone, which was crucial for them to know the intended victim's movements.

Penny saw him come out of the station and go to his car, and then followed him out of the car park. She banged the wheel in frustration when he took a different turn, obviously not going by the route they wanted. She called Anne and then Jane to tell them that it was off.

It was a dispirited group that made its way back to London that afternoon saying that they would try again the next week. On the way back, Jane stopped at a call box and put through a call to the States and gave the code word to Francis, which in effect, gave her another week there. Francis then sent a telegram to Stephen saying that she was staying for an extra week.

So the following Friday, Jane was hidden up in the copse, Anne was waiting in Jane's car, parked on the side of the same road from Chelmsford and Penny was in the station car park. She perked up when he came out of the station, and as the week before, followed him out of the car park. This time, he took the road they wanted! At her designated point, Penny phoned Anne and told her it was a go, then alerted Jane of the same.

Anne put the phone down and got out of the car, and then started to walk along the road. It was a nice hot summer's day and she had taken off her panties and left them in the car. Her only clothing was a short halter top, without a bra beneath it, and a very short skirt and a pair of shoes. She walked along the country road for at least a quarter of a mile before she heard the car coming up from behind.

Anne turned and stepped out into the middle of the road, jumping up and down and waving her arms. The short halter top she was wearing as she jumped about, showed it was evident that she wasn't wearing a bra. Her full breasts bounced about and the lower curve of them could be seen quite clearly.

Stephen brought the car to a halt and Anne jauntily bounced her way to him. Her breasts were doing exactly what they were intended to, and that was to attract his attention.

'Could you give me a lift into the village, please? My car broke down and it's still a long walk.' Her smile was sweet and seductive. He remembered passing a car by the side of the road and surmised that that was the car she was referring to.

'No problem,' he said, 'jump in.' He watched her get in, and was sure that he had seen a bit of muff as her legs had parted to get in the car.

'We could go back for me to have a look at it, if you want?' he said.

'Oh, don't bother! It's my brother's stupid car. I'll tell him where it is and he can come and fix it.' She gave Stephen a sweet smile. 'Let's just get going.'

He put the car into gear and started off. 'Better put your seat belt on,' he said.

'Oh I can't bear those things. It squashes my tits,' was Anne's saucy reply. 'Look!' and she made a show of the belt pushing her big tits apart.

Stephen had already begun to sweat. Her short skirt had ridden a little up her legs and he could see the upper parts of her thighs, but just not enough to be sure if she was without panties. He felt himself getting aroused.

'Phew! It's bloody hot today, isn't it?' she asked, her hands flapping the lower part of her top. 'Do you live round here? I used to. I used to come out on this road and go to the river for a swim every summer. Do you know it? We used to go skinny dipping, and I still do when I get the chance. Do you ever go skinny dipping?'

'No,' was the reply.

'Oh you should try it. It's fantastic! Everything floating free in the water. There!' She pointed, 'It's just down there, down that track. Do come, please?' He shook his head, but he had slowed the car down.

'Well let me go for a quick dip. I'm so hot and sweaty,' she paused, 'in all the right places. You can watch if you want,' she said slyly. That was enough. He swung off the road and followed the track down to the trees.

'He's taken the bait,' Penny said to Jane from her phone, following half a mile behind. 'Be ready.'

Stephen drove the car down the bumpy track as Anne directed and pulled up under the trees by the river. Anne was quickly out of the car and ran past a small rickety bridge, to a spot beneath a great big oak. Here she turned and waited for him to come to her. Anne stood there, her hands up under her top, obviously caressing the breasts beneath.

'Are you sure you won't join me?' she asked, taking his hands.

'No. I'll just watch, as you said.'

'Well sit down here,' she pulled him to a fallen trunk and pushed him down to sit. Then she moved back and then slowly pulled her halter over her head. Her breasts, taut and upstanding, were revealed to him as she pulled it off. Then with a smile, her fingers undid the clip of her skirt and let it fall. He found he was fully aroused as she revealed the tidy bush between her thighs.

This was the last thing he saw as Jane crashed a heavy round stone to the top of his head.

Jane had watched the car turn off the road and approach the trees and then concealed herself in the bushes. When Anne had sat him down and started to strip, she moved up behind him and dealt him the knockout blow. She dropped the stone and looked at Anne, standing naked there before her instead of watching Stephen crumple at her feet. She orgasmed, but was not sure if that was due to looking at Anne there in all her glory, or the fact she had just possibly killed the man at her feet.

It was difficult for her to move as Anne came over and knelt down next to Stephen. 'Come on,' she said urgently.

With the wetness between her thighs and the shakiness of her legs, it was hard for Jane to bend down and grab the shoulders of the man while Anne lifted up his legs. They carried him to the river and tossed him in. Anne then went into the river and sat on the body that was face down.

'Hurry up,' she said, 'this water is bloody freezing.' Jane then hurried off to the rickety bridge, picking up a large branch as she did so. With this branch, she smashed it down on the frail rail, splitting it in two. Then with her gloved hands, brushed away any remaining bark from the break.

Throwing away this branch, she then went and gave a wave to Penny, waiting up on the road in her car. Then back to the river, pausing to heave the stone she had used into the river and to help Anne out of the cold water.

Anne had been sitting on Stephen's body, face down in the water while Jane broke the balustrade of the bridge. Now very cold indeed, she pushed the body out into the slow flow of the river and used Jane's hand to help her out onto the bank, stepping out onto the towels Jane had laid out for her. When clear of the bank, she started to rub herself dry and didn't object when Jane gave her a hand, nor notice where the hands went.

Penny pulled up at the edge of the trees and the two girls scampered out and into the car. Penny turned the car round and drove back up the track and out onto the road.

'How did it go?' she enquired.

'Just as we planned. To the letter!' said Jane, 'Anne looked beautiful back there in the trees. He couldn't take his eyes off her when she undressed.'

'It was so exciting! I've never done anything like that before,' said Anne, her voice conveying the thrill that it had been for her. 'But that water was bloody cold!'

Penny drove on till they reached Jane's car, where Jane got out from Penny's and climbed into hers.

'Anne?' Jane called out. 'Do you want a lift home? I can go past your place.' Anne said okay and got out of Penny's car. Penny caught her hand.

'Take care, Anne,' she said softly.

'I will,' and she gave Penny a brief kiss on the cheek. 'See you later.'

'I meant with Jane,' she said softly under her breath as Anne got into Jane's car. She followed Jane's car to Chelmsford where with a toot of the horn, the two cars parted company.

'You did well back there, Anne,' Jane said, 'especially when he saw this.' Her left hand flicked up the skirt of Anne to show the hair between her thighs. 'Then these breasts of yours,' her hand then brushed the nipples that were prominently showing through the thin fabric of the top.

'I...I can't explain it. I actually got a sexual thrill from showing my body like that. It's the first time I've ever done anything like that, and it was....it was exciting.'

Jane let it drop there and concentrated on getting Anne to her home as quickly as possible. She didn't need to be told the directions and it didn't register that Jane obviously knew where she lived. She parked the car by the side of the road, one cottage down from Anne's and walked back to the cottage with her.

'Can I come in for a drink?' Jane asked, 'I could really do with one.'

'Of course,' Anne said, opening the door and letting them both inside the cottage. They sat there, opposite each other with their drinks in hand.

'Did you really get a thrill there in the trees?' Jane asked.

'Oh yes. It was wonderful. I got some kind of sexual thrill out of it.'

'Would you like to experience it again?'

'How?'

'By us going through it again. I'll pretend to be Stephen and we can act it out again to see if you get the same thrill. I'm sure I will.'

'You felt it too?'

'You do not know how much. You were wonderful in that performance. So much so, that I would like to see it again.'

'You would?'

'Yes, please.'

'Well I've led you to the tree trunk and you've sat down, right? Then I took of my top very slowly, like this.' She slowly pulled the top up so that her full breasts were very taut as she took it off.

'Then I undid the clip of my skirt and let it fall to the ground.' Which she did as she spoke. 'And then you were behind him and hit him.'

Jane looked at the full naked body of Anne standing there, and mentally licked her lips.

'But what if he had got up before I could hit him. Like this,' she said, standing up and moved across to Anne.

'What if he had taken your arm and led you back to the fallen tree and sat you down on his lap.' Jane was doing this very action as she spoke, 'and then put his hand upon your breast like this.' Her hand cupped Anne's full breast and gently moved her hand on it.

'I...I...don't know. It wasn't supposed to happen.'

'Then he might have put it here.' Her hand left the breast and went between Anne's legs.

'No, no,' she pushed Jane's hand away and got up, shaking, 'it couldn't have happened that way.' Her voice was trembling as she moved across the room and gathered up her skirt and put it on. 'You would have hit him before he did anything like that.'

Anne put her top on as well and quickly drained her glass. 'I...I think you'd better go now,' she said, voice still shaky.

Jane gave her a slow smile and finished off her drink.

'Yes I'd better just do that. Thanks for the drink and I'll see you later.'

After she had gone, Anne poured herself another drink and sat down in a chair, her legs still trembling. She'd nearly fallen for it. She'd liked the hand on her breast, but it was the quickness of that finger sliding up into her innermost part that brought her to her senses. If Jane had been a bit more patient and progressed slower, she might have gone along with it. But, she said to herself, she'd rather have a man's hard thing up there than a woman's finger. She didn't feel like cooking any dinner for herself, so she just finished the drink and went for a bath before going to bed.

Penny, as she drove home alone, wondered if Jane would get her way with Anne, and if she did, how would it affect the group? Believing she would find out soon enough, she put it from her mind. There were still two to go, one of them being her William.

So she went over the rough plans she had in her mind for the rest of the way home.

***

FRANCIS ARRIVED at the airport on Tuesday evening and said to hell with trains, and lashed out on a taxi to take her home. The house was in darkness and Stephen's car wasn't in the drive. She went in and made herself a sandwich and fixed a drink and sat down in the kitchen to consume them. She had been tingling all the way from the airport, and now was pretty sure that the girls had done the deed, with the house being as empty as it was.

Forewarned about this by Jane, that there was a strong possibility that he might not be found by the time she got home, so she was to remain calm. She then followed the advice that Penny had given her. Think logically. You come home; he's not there. He might have mistook the date and was staying somewhere else for the night. Wait till the morning before phoning his office, asking to speak to him.

This she did, waiting till after ten before ringing his office. A female voice answered, and on hearing the query, replied that he was not in, and hadn't been in Monday or Tuesday either.

Francis then asked to be put through to his immediate superior, and when the connection was made, asked if her husband had been sent out on some particular job, or whatever. With the answer being in the negative, she explained that she had arrived home from the States the previous evening, but found that her husband wasn't there to greet her. His car was not there either, she added, putting a little hysteria into her voice. The voice at the other end of the phone, upon hearing this, tried to calm her. He told her to ring the police, not wanting to put into words that her husband might have had an accident, which was what he must have been thinking.

She broke the connection and rang up the local police station, saying that she had been advised to, that her husband appeared to be missing. She told them the same story, and they said they would send somebody round.

It was nearly three hours later that a small police car pulled up at the front door. Francis had it open as a young policeman and policewoman got out of the car. She was wringing her hands together as she waited for them to approach her. They all went inside and she told them that she had been visiting her daughter in the States and had come home to an empty house. She also phoned his place of work, but they hadn't seen him since last Friday, and it was now late Wednesday afternoon. No, she hadn't phoned the hospital, in any case, which one should she have phoned? The one in Chelmsford, or any of those in between there and London? She made herself become quite hysterical and the policewoman calmed her down, saying that they would do the checking for her.

So he was reported missing.

It was Friday morning when she saw the policewoman come up to the door to give her the news that her husband had been found. The officer wouldn't give any details, only that he'd been found dead in a river. Francis broke down. The policewoman tried to comfort her, even as she explained that distressing as it was, Francis would still have to identify the body.

It was a nerve-wracking experience and the autopsy showed that his death was due to drowning. The blow to the head was put down to his falling from the bridge, and being rendered unconscious, drowned. The verdict was accidental death.

He was buried a week later.

***

PENNY GAVE Francis three weeks before contacting her through their mail system, and when they met, she wasn't sure what to say until Francis thanked her for freeing her to start life again.

Pleased with this, Penny went on to tell her of the plan in respect of her role in seeing to William Swithers.

Francis agreed and was therefore in London every Monday until Tuesday morning. This first Monday, they went over the plan once again with Anne and Jane, and they all went and saw the flat that had been rented and Francis made her move that very evening.

Francis couldn't help but laugh afterwards. It was so easy to snare William Swithers. She might have been thirty-nine years of age, but she still had more knowledge of how to handle a man than girls half her age did.

She was in his favourite haunt before him, sitting at a table, wait-ing. He entered with two of his male friends and sat down on a stool at the bar. Fortunately, he sat at the end of the three and not in the middle, otherwise she would have had to wait till later. But he was placed exactly for what she had in mind. A full pint was in front of him when she went up to the bar and ordered a Bloody Mary. When it came, she paid the barman and with an adroit movement, managed to turn and knock his pint of beer into his lap, and at the same time, send her own drink down the front of her white blouse.

Profuse apologies were spilled out, and using a bar cloth in her hand, she tried to mop the front of his trousers, whilst trying to wipe the front of her blouse. Being bra-less, her attempts to wipe herself only pressed the wet, red stained blouse tighter across her breasts, making the nipples beneath stand out more prominently.

'Look, I can only apologise, but I'll make it up to you and buy you another beer or two, but I'm soaking wet and so are you. I've just moved into a flat that's literally just round the corner. Why don't you come with me while I change and at least try to dry your trousers? Then I will buy you another drink afterwards.'

With a laugh and a quick joke to his friends, he followed Francis out of the bar and taking her arm, asked how far away was her flat. They'd left the bar and turned left in the King's Road and took the first turning on the left, and he'd only just finished asking the question when she pointed that they were there already. This was the flat that Penny had rented with the aid of the birth certificate. She had already taken the trouble to make it look as though it was lived in; food, crockery, things around the small lounge. Also, the flat had a made up bed and a wardrobe full of clothes and a bathroom full of toiletries and towels.

Francis used her key for the front door, which led into the foyer, and they went up one flight of stairs to the flat. Another key let them inside, and she led him straight down the hall and into the bedroom.

'I must get out of this sticky blouse,' she said over her shoulder, going past the bed and into the bathroom. 'My name's Ruth, by the way,' she called out. This being the name on the rental papers. 'What's yours?'

'William,' he called out, moving round the bed, and then stopping when he could see her reflection in the full length mirror of the bathroom. Francis had just taken off her blouse and he could see her full breasts quite clearly, then the triangle of hair as she dropped her skirt and panties.

'I won't be a minute,' she shouted above the shower water's noise that she had just turned on. 'I'll just get this yuk off and be right with you. Make yourself comfortable.'

Being the man he was, he couldn't help but be aroused as he had watched her strip and get into the shower. He took his jacket off and threw it onto a chair and then took off his trousers and underpants. He waited till the water was turned off and she had started to dry herself on a large towel before he walked into the bathroom with his trousers over his arm and his arousal very evident and to be seen below the front of his shirt.

'Wow,' she gasped as she saw him standing there before her. 'Someone's pleased to see me,' she said looking at his naked lower half, but holding her towel in front of herself. 'I didn't mean get that comfortable,' she teased with a little laugh. 'I haven't seen a sight like that for three years now. Not since my husband died.'

'My god, you're beautiful,' he said, moving close up to her and dropping his trousers as he pulled the towel away from her hands. He looked her up and down.

'That's why you can see what I've got. So it's been three years you've gone without it? With that body I can't imagine why!'

Francis managed to look coy as he moved closer still and took her in his arms, his manhood sliding up her stomach as he held her close and buried his face into her neck as he kissed her there. Her hand went slowly to his shoulders and she moved her feet slightly so that what he had rubbed between them.

'What about your trousers?' she whispered.

'Sod the trousers,' he said, transferring his kisses to her lips as he turned her round and moved her backwards out of the bathroom till they fell onto the bed.

***

"WHAT ABOUT that drink I promised you,' she said softly as she cradled his head against her breast after having an hour of expert loving from him.

'I'll take that drink here,' he murmured as he began moving down her body as he kissed her.

***

OH WHY are you getting rid of him, Penny? Francis thought. He's fantastic as she had another orgasm. But then she remembered Penny had said that everybody but her was getting it from him.

It was another hour later and they were both dressed when he asked if he could see her again. Francis explained that the only evenings she had free were Mondays, as she was over at a friend's place every evening for studying. It took some little argument, but she got her way and they agreed to meet the next Monday, but at a different bar. She said that she didn't like drinking on her own doorstep.

Penny knew that contact had been established by the fact that William's trousers were badly crumpled and he had gone for a shower as soon as he had arrived in their bedroom. Also that with just after a few words between them, he fell asleep. She grinned as she settled herself down for the night too.

***

FRANCIS MET William in a bar of her choice the following Monday where they had a drink before going to a small Italian restaurant for dinner. Then it was back to Francis's flat where he spent the night. After doing it twice, she was cuddled up to him and said that next week, she would like to be taken to a theatre before dinner. This he agreed to, so the girls were advised to be in their positions at the appointed time.

On Friday, Penny left London and flew to Paris for the week to visit with some friends.

Monday night arrived and again William met Francis, in a different bar this time. They went up to a theatre in Leicester Square and after the show, had dinner. He didn't notice that Francis was clock watching, and at the right time, she suggested they went home. On leaving the restaurant, she hugged his arm and said that she wanted to go by tube. He objected, but she got her way, and dragged him down to the underground station. It was only a couple of stops, he argued, but laughingly agreed to her whim.

Francis checked her watch while he got the tickets and she took her time getting down to their platform so that they arrived just as one was leaving. William remarked on them missing it, but she said that there would be another along in a few minutes.

She wandered down the platform till she was about four carriage lengths from the tunnel entrance and then stood near the edge. William suggested that they move back a bit, but she pointed out that the station was filling up fast, this being the last train. He looked round and saw that in just the few minutes that they had been down there, the platform was almost filled up with people anxious not to miss this train.

Francis had seen Anne and Jane move up close behind them so it was time for her to get out a small bunch of keys. These she juggled in her hand, tossing them up a little way, and catching them as they fell. She could hear the train approach, and as she saw the lights approaching the exit from the tunnel, she dropped the keys at his feet. It was an automatic reaction on William's part, to bend down to pick them up.

The train burst from the tunnel with its loud roar as William's hand touched the keys. People were moving about and swaying and he was nudged on the shoulder and on the hip at the same time. They were quite hard nudges. Hard enough to send him off balance and off the edge of the platform.

There were screams from several women further up the platform as the front of the train struck him, hurling him forward and down beneath the wheels. The screeching of the brakes drowned out the screaming women and the shouting of many people. The area from where he had fallen was suddenly clear, a semicircle of empty platform.

Francis had melted back into the crowd, and Anne and Jane weren't to be seen anywhere. Many people left the station knowing that that train wouldn't be leaving for quite a while. Francis was among them.

The ghouls and attention seekers were the only people to stay, all claiming to be witnesses so that they could see the ambulance men retrieve the body of William from the track. He fell, was pushed, suffered stomach cramps and slipped, jumped and the witnesses described many more ways as to how William Swithers met his end.

Francis was gathered up by the girls a little way from the station where they had been looking out for her. They walked a little way and went into a crowded bar.

'I needed that!' said Francis as she drank her large gin and tonic, straight down and ordered another. Anne and Jane followed suit.

'I didn't like doing this one,' she whispered, tears in her eyes, 'I was becoming attached to him.'

'But it wouldn't have lasted long,' Jane said, 'well, that's according to Penny.'

'What do we do now?' Anne asked. 'We can't meet at Penny's anymore.'

'We just have to wait at home until she contacts us,' Francis said, knocking back half of her second drink.

'On the Internet you mean,' interrupted Jane.

'You know what I meant,' Francis said testily. 'I do know that she wants to know the date of the next race meeting at Warwick?' looking at Jane.

'That's in about six weeks' time. Is that when she wants to do it?' Jane asked, her hand still trembling from what she had done at the station. Francis nodded as she finished her drink and ordered another round.

'She's found a hotel just off the M25 at Heathrow for the job. Look, Jane. You don't really want to hear this. The less you know the better. All you've got to do is make sure your man goes to that meeting. Give Penny the date of the last day of the meeting, and you can be away off on your cruise till it's all over.'

'You're right! I don't want to know.' She finished her drink and giving each girl a kiss on the cheek, said goodbye, and left the bar to go home leaving Anne and Francis in the bar.

'Now Penny told me before she went off, what she had got planned. This was because she would have to be careful when she came back,' said Francis, then telling Anne of their roles in the rubbing out of Jane's husband.

'So it's just a matter of waiting till Penny gives us the go ahead,' Francis finished off.

'When did she sort all this out?' Anne asked.

'Weeks ago. She's been scouring round hotels to find one that would fit the bill. Also she knew that she wouldn't be as free as she was on this night. For a few weeks at least,' she added.

'That's why she told me exactly how it could be carried out. So we just wait for her to say go.'

With that, they finished their drinks and because of the lateness of the night with their last train having already left, went to the flat in Chelsea for the night, leaving the following morning.

***

PENNY DULY landed at Heathrow on Friday and was soon back in her house in Knightsbridge. It was no different to any other homecoming. Her husband wasn't at home, though she didn't expect him to be this time, if the girls' had done their business, because he had never really been at home any other time she had been away. He'd always had the excuse that he'd had an important client that he couldn't let down. But he could always let me down, was the bitter thought of Penny. Though this time she could excuse him for not being there. In fact she welcomed the fact that he wasn't there. That, if all had gone well, he wouldn't have been able to.

So it was now just a matter of waiting till the police arrived to break the bad news to her, the news that he wouldn't ever be coming home. With the taxi driver placing her bags in the hall and accepting the generous tip, she went into the kitchen and mixed herself a strong drink and sat down at the table.

The police arrived just after ten the next morning to tell her of her husband's accident. She did her upper class act of keeping an equally stiff lip, and concealing her true feelings at the news of the tragic accident that had befallen him.

'That's a true sign of good breeding,' said the young constable that accompanied the W.P.C. 'Taking the news of her husband's death like that. Tight lipped and not showing her true emotions. That's class!'

The W.P.C. looked askance at him, keeping her own council of thoughts to herself.

Two days later, Penny checked her E-mail and saw that she had a message from number one, Anne. It read, *"Money in. What next? Same message sent number three. Will monitor daily.* " Penny sent back, *"Suggest we meet at flat next Thursday at noon,"* and sent one to Jane and Francis too.

They had already prepared for this and had visited several warehouses that had been converted into storage cubicles of different sizes that could be rented by the month and had selected those that they could use.

Penny was waiting in the flat for them as they all had agreed to the meeting and Anne got a kiss on the cheek being the first to arrive.

'Isn't it wonderful?' Anne gushed. 'Six hundred and eighty thousand pounds! I can't wait to tell the others,' and she gave Penny a big hug. They went through to the kitchen and had a glass of wine as they prepared a snack lunch for the others before they arrived. Which they did, both at the same time.

It was a peck on the cheek for everyone as they met and Penny led them through to the kitchen where they kissed and hugged Anne at the wonderful news when she said how much she had received. More wine was poured out and they all sat down at the kitchen table.

'The square circle meets again. Before you say anything, I've brought you all back a souvenir from Paris,' Penny said as she passed over to them, a small flat box each. They eagerly opened the exquisitely done up parcels to reveal that they had a silk head scarf each.

'It's gorgeous,' Anne exclaimed. 'Look, they're all the same,' she said as she compared it to Jane's.

'So's mine,' Penny said, pleased that they liked the small gifts she had brought. 'Now, how did it go with William?'

'I was pretty scared in the crush at the station,' Anne said, 'but felt exhilarated afterwards. It was pandemonium trying to get out from the platform without being noticed, and the reaction didn't set in till we went and had a drink.'

'Well they seem to have bought it, for the newspapers report it as being an accident,' Jane said, 'but we'll have to wait for the coroner's inquest. How do you feel in yourself Penny?'

'I feel wonderful! You will too when we, er, set you free,' Penny replied. 'Now let's eat lunch and we can talk about what's next.'

They bustled about to get the prepared meal from the fridge and replenished their glasses as Jane spoke again.

'Now we must start the next stages in respect of the money that Anne now has and what you Francis and Penny will shortly be getting. Here's what we do,' Jane started, picking up her fork and taking small mouthfuls of food whilst explaining to the others. After lunch, they would go to one of the storage places they had selected, and Anne was to ask to rent one of their small containers. The explanation being that she wanted to keep some of her recently deceased mother's effects in a safe place.

Penny passed across the rental agreement she had acquired plus the birth certificate for Anne to use as identification. The name on it was for Ruth Richards, and she had the flat rental papers to show as her living address.

Anne was then, at a time of her choosing, to go to her bank and start to withdraw the money out over the next two weeks and put this money in a suitcase to be placed in the depository that she had rented. When this was done, she was to pass over the rental agreement and birth certificate for Penny to keep till either she or Francis needed it next. Anne was to keep the key to the lock-up on her house key ring, and not to lose it.

So with lunch over, they washed up the things and put them away before they went off to the depository selected, passing over the wig from Francis to Anne to put on before entering. Everything went off without a hitch, and the papers were signed and Anne said that she would be bringing some things along later. The address was noted from the rental agreement as being just off the King's Road, and the phone number.

The next step was to stop and buy four suitcases for the carrying and transferring of the money from the banks. With this done, they stopped at a wine bar for a drink, and Jane said to the others that they should meet in two weeks' time, same time at the flat. Anne was to have got the insurance money from her bank and placed in the lock-up by that time. Penny would then tell them of the plan that she had devised and put forward for Jane's husband and their respective roles in its execution. Also that they would set up the other depositories at the same time.

They parted for their respective homes and the following day, Anne started to make her withdrawals of the money from the bank. The manager was much distressed at her taking so much out of the account and she was very apprehensive at taking this money home. Jane also began making her enquiries about taking her mini cruise during the three-day race meeting at Warwick.

In the time frame, Anne cleared the insurance money from her account and with it all packed into the suitcase, placed it in the depository on her way to the flat for their next meeting. She was the first again at the flat where Penny was waiting and only arrived a few minutes before the other two.

'Cheers,' said Jane lifting her glass of wine to salute the others seated round the table. 'Just my one to go. I'm all butterflies now. How are you going to do it? The Warwick meeting is only two weeks away.'

'That is what you are not going to know!' said Penny most emphatically. 'It has to be a surprise to you when you are told, so that part we can't tell you. We'll talk about it after you've left to go and get your tickets for the cruise you wanted to take. Is the insurance money in the lock up, Anne?'

'Yes. The bank manager didn't like me taking it all out,' she said with a nervous laugh.

'Okay, let's have lunch so that Jane can go off after while we discuss the plan I've devised.'

So with lunch sorted out and eaten, Jane left and told Anne and Francis of what they would be doing in respect of Jane's husband. After this, they went out and visited three more depositories and booked the smallest they had, Penny putting on a wig to rent out one for Jane. It was a successful day all told and it was agreed that it was a go for the last day of the Warwick race meeting.

At the inquest of William Swithers, Penny, dressed in mourning, sat through the proceedings and bowed her head at the coroner's verdict of accidental death.

***

IT HAD taken some time to find the right location for the seeing to of Michael Pound. The ideal place that fitted her plan was a high rise hotel just outside of Heathrow Airport. It was a three-day meeting and Jane had sailed on her cruise two days before it opened. She had given Penny some tips on horses to follow at the meeting and this is what she had to rely on.

Penny played a flirtatious part over the three days, losing small amounts to Michael Pound, but hitting him with big bets on the tips she had. They paid off rather handsomely. By the second day, she had him meeting her in the bar after the racing for drinks and she kept teasing him about how much money she was going to win off him. He tried to bed her on that day, without success, but on the last day, she said that he could get his money's worth back if he would take her to heaven.

'And just where is this ideal heaven you are looking for?' Michael Pound asked Penny in the bar before the start of this last day's racing.

Penny in not only taking tips on the horses running at Warwick, but on also just the kind of women he picked up. The mode of dress and slightly overdone make-up, the skirt being a bit too short and the blouse or whatever, a size too small and definitely not to wear a bra. She sipped at the drink he had bought for her and smiled coyly over the rim.

'The Heathrow Hilton is on the way home. It's high and I like to see and hear the power of jet planes taking off. The throb of the power as it sits on the tarmac, it slowly building up until the brakes are released and it begins to move faster and faster before exploding in one final surge as it takes off, whisking one away to heaven.' He caught the analogy and couldn't wait until the meeting was over to be that aircraft and take her to heaven.

Much to his annoyance, Penny still managed to get four winners out of six, blowing him a kiss each time she collected her winnings. In spite of this, he'd still made a good profit out of the meeting and now in the bar after the last race, he was anxious to get going to the hotel where he could at least get something in return for the money Penny had won off him. He eyed the cleavage of her full breasts and was already aroused with his thoughts for the night to come.

They had already collected their bags from their respective hotels in Warwick and with his assistant driving, made their way towards the M40. She had deliberately dallied in the bar at the racecourse so that when they arrived at the hotel she had chosen, it was dark.

She had allowed him to play with her breasts in the back of the car just to get him most anxious to bed her. As they pulled into the car park of the hotel outside of the airport, Penny was relieved to see her car still there where she had parked it and that Francis and Anne were inside it.

Michael's assistant got her suitcase out of the car and was told to go off home for he would get a taxi in the morning. He began to walk to the hotel, when she stopped him, really waiting for his car to leave the hotel car park.

'You go in first Michael,' she said, 'and book a room as high as you can get. The higher we will be to heaven just adds to the thrill and excitement. I'll follow and wait by the lift.'

Francis had already gotten out of the car and began to walk towards Penny as he departed.

'Quick. Put the case in the car and come into the lobby and the lifts as quick as you can,' she said and Francis almost ran to the car with Penny's case, Anne having got out had the boot open ready. They then quickly followed Penny into the hotel though staying quite a few steps behind her.

Penny saw him checking in at the desk and went over to the lifts to wait for him. Such was his eagerness to get her up to the room, he never noticed that she didn't have her suitcase with her. He hurried over to the lifts where she was waiting once he'd got his key and didn't take any notice of the two women that had followed and stood behind and entered the lift after he and Penny had got inside.

'What room are we in, darling?' Penny asked him, taking his arm in hers.

'Six two four,' he said and Penny looked over his shoulder and saw Francis give a nod.

'What floor do you want?' Penny asked the other two in the lift with them.

'Seventh please,' Francis answered and so Penny pressed the floors six and seven. Her and Michael got out at the sixth floor and walked slowly down the carpeted corridor to their room. He opened the door and she went inside with him following, closing the door behind him. Penny went straight to the French windows and opened them to the miniscule balcony that she knew was there.

'This is as high as I could get,' he said as she looked out to see that they were off to the side of the main entrance and above the car park.

'Perfect Michael, just perfect,' she said as she turned from the window and went to the mini bar and got out a small whisky and emptied it into a glass which she handed to him. As she was dressed a bit more sombrely in travelling clothes, he took no notice that she was wearing gloves. He took the drink and sat down on the small chair the room provided as she went off towards the door.

'Where are you going?' he asked, sipping at his drink.

'To put the Do Not Disturb sign on the outside of the door,' she said, pulling it off the inside door handle and then opened the door.

She saw Anne and Francis outside as she slipped the notice on the outside and mouthed the word five to them and was careful not to close the door properly. She walked back to the bed and pulled the top covers right back and began to take her clothes off.

'Come and get your winnings now,' she said as she finished and laid herself out completely naked, her head towards to window. He quickly gulped down the rest of his drink and began taking his clothes off at seeing her lying there waiting for him. He moved round as he took them off and had his back to the small passage way from the door to the room and when naked himself, up and ready for action, paused for a moment before covering her body with his.

He didn't see, but Penny did over his shoulder, Anne and Francis move into the room and he had actually entered her when he was suddenly seized by the arms and roughly pulled up off and out of Penny.

'What the hell?' he spluttered at this sudden intrusion as he was pulled to his feet. That was all he had time to say for Penny was up just as quick and drove her fist into his midriff which blew all the air out of his body. He began to double over as he was hustled out from that side of the bed and was then suddenly propelled towards the open French windows. He couldn't see it coming, being doubled up as he was, only being held up by the two pair of hands either side of him that moved him across the carpeted room.

He was still trying to get some breath into his lungs when the run stopped and the hands let go of him with a push and he suddenly was at and over the small balcony rail. He didn't scream for he hadn't the breath as he hurtled through the air for six stories and died instantly with a broken neck as he landed on the tarmac of the car park, fortunately for the car owners below, he landed between two of them.

He was still in the air as Penny stripped off the lower bed sheet and taking a clean fresh one from the plastic bag that Anne had carried in. One that Penny had stolen a week ago and now began remaking the bed. Francis came and took over with Anne for Penny to get dressed.

She checked over the bed that it looked perfect as Francis put the sheet she had lain on in the plastic bag. Anne looked wistfully at his bookmaker's bag that she knew was full of money. She would have loved to have taken it but it had to be left behind.

It took them three minutes to be out of the room and they slowly, one at a time, crossed the lobby and escaped out to where Penny's car was parked. She opened the doors for them but still had to move along the parked cars to find his body and make sure he was dead. It only took one look at the angle of his head to know that it was so before going back and getting into the car, drove them off out for London.

Michael Pound's body wasn't found till eight o'clock next morning by a guest departing. Police and an ambulance were summonsed and two hours later, his body was in the morgue. The autopsy, three hours later confirmed that he had died from a broken neck due to a fight with gravity. The body contained a quantity of alcohol and it was assumed that this was the cause of him falling off the sixth floor balcony. Accidental death was noted by the police. Suicide had been ruled out for his bag showed that he had made enough money. Murder too, for the money would surely have been stolen if this was the case.

Jane broke down into tears when she was informed of his death after the return from her cruise, silently rejoicing for only she knew the secret of the money he had been hiding from the tax man.

The very next week Francis was paid out her insurance money which a week later she removed from the bank in cash and placed in her lock up in its suitcase. Two months later, Penny received hers and another month saw Jane get hers. All being lodged in their respective depositories lockers. Soon they would get together for the share out minus expenses of course.

But things took a turn for the worse before this could happen.

***

"I'M FRIGHTENED,' came the voice over the phone. 'I think I'm being followed.'

'But….'

'No names or numbers,' came the scared voice. 'Look. We must meet and talk. You know the station two up from where you normally get the train for London?'

'Yes.'

'Well, from the left as you come out, about two hundred yards along there's a bridge. Meet me there in two hours. I'll be watching to see that you aren't being followed. Wear a dark coat.'

'But….'

'See you in two hours,' and the line went dead. Puzzled and alarmed, she did as she was told and got out a dark top coat and making sure the front door was locked, left the house and hurried to the station. She hurried because she didn't know the times of the trains in that direction and so would rather be early than late. Besides, it would give her a chance to see if anybody was following her too.

She bought her return ticket to Edgewood station and sat down on the platform and fretted. She sat there for forty minutes with all kinds of thoughts running through her mind, none of which made sense and was relieved when the train finally pulled in.

She got off at Edgewood station and only saw one other person alight from the train and was thankful that they turned right on leaving the station. She hurried off to the left towards the bridge where her friend was waiting for her. The woman on the bridge watched her leave the station and come up to the bridge and approached to where she was standing almost on the opposite side.

'Did anyone follow you?' she gasped to her waiting friend, slightly out of breath for hurrying.

'No, but I think you were followed, look!'

She turned her head to look back along the way she had come and didn't see the fist coming that crashed into her jaw. The blow rendered her almost unconscious and she staggered back to the wall of the bridge and was then held upright by her assailant. She was unaware of the hand going through the pockets of her coat, or of the handbag pulled from her grasp. It was only when the rings were being pulled from her left hand finger that she started to move but was hit again. She was roughly turned round so that her face lay against the cold damp bricks of the bridge wall and felt her legs being grasped and she was lifted up.

She tried to get her brain in gear as her upper body was lying across the top of the parapet and realised that things were going wrong for her. She didn't have much time to try and reason why for her ankles were suddenly grasped and lifted up so that the whole of her body went over the top.

She bounced on the metal shield above the electrified wire that passed below it and then touched it. Body being earthed, there was a big blue flash and she died instantly from being electrocuted. Her body then fell down onto the track as the other figure on the bridge, picked up the handbag and made her way to the station. She calmly walked out onto the platform with her return ticket she had already purchased some hours before and watched as the nonstop express roared through before her train came.

The contents of the handbag were slowly disposed of, the empty bag finally finished up in a skip. The rings had been dropped down various drains and any papers were later cut up and flushed down the toilet. The only thing kept was the key to the depository locker.

It was just getting light when the motorman of a train coming up from London saw a bundle on the opposite track and when he stopped at Edgewood station, told the station foreman of it about fifty yards the other side of the bridge. After this train had pulled out to continue its journey, the station foreman went down onto the tracks and walked along the line on the opposite side.

He knew what he was going to find later when he saw the severed foot beside the line just below the bridge and only approached the bundle close enough to assume rightly as it happened, that it was indeed the body of a woman. He hurried back to the station and called the police and informed the railway's control centre that he had a body on the line and so the signal lights went to red on that sector of the line. It caused disruption but it couldn't be helped.

Not only did the police turn up but an ambulance as well and there were four policemen and two paramedics soon scrambling down the embankment on the far side of the bridge to find that it was indeed a woman. One policeman was sick on the spot when he saw the damage done to a human face after being dragged over fifty yards by a train on the rough stones and sleepers.

Half an hour later they had police photographers taking pictures of not only the body but of the severed foot and other pictures of the scene before the paramedics were allowed to remove the body from the track. It was only when they went to move it did they find that the left arm had been torn from the torso and it wasn't to be found even though two constables walked nearly three miles up the track and back again.

It was decided that all trains that had passed along that line in the last twenty four hours be checked and it wasn't until five o'clock that evening that the severed left arm was found wedged up in the bogie wheels of a carriage of the London express. Three hours later it was reunited with the rest of the body in the morgue, labelled as an unidentified Caucasian female person of middle years. The autopsy would be left till the next day.

Meanwhile, during the day at about the same time as the body was being removed from the railway line, a suitcase was removed from one depository locker to be placed alongside an identical one in another depository.

***

"**I'M FRIGHTENED,**' came the same whispered voice over the phone that night. 'I tried contacting….no, no names or numbers. I think I'm being watched and maybe followed. I've given them the slip to phone you from a phone box.'

'What's happened?' came the anguished question.

'I don't know,' the voice wailed from the other end. 'We got to meet to sort this out, please, I need help.'

'Where are you?' was the crisp reply.

'I daren't say over the phone. Do you remember the viaduct where we stopped once because of the lovely view?'

'Yes.'

'Meet me there in four hours' time. We've got to sort this out and see if we went wrong somewhere.'

'Why can't we meet at...?'

'No! No names please, I begging you, please come,' the voice at the other end of the phone pleaded.

'Okay, four hours' time.'

'Wear something dark for it'll be nighttime. You'll be harder to follow if that's the case.' The line went dead and she thought that something must be wrong for her to be panicky like this and went and put on a pair of stout walking shoes for she knew she would have to walk for nearly half an hour to reach the viaduct for the meeting point.

There were no lights on this stretch of road and it was only lit by starlight as she approached the rendezvous and could just ascertain the solitary figure there waiting for her. She quickened her pace and was soon up close to her.

'Now tell me what's caused this panic? You sounded so...so distraught.'

'Tell me you weren't followed,' she begged.

'No, I wasn't.'

'Then who is that?'

It was the same trick being pulled as at the railway bridge. Of course she turned her head to look and was hit in the same way. Only this time, the blow knocked her round and so that she was already half over the stone parapet. Again the pockets were divested of what they contained for she hadn't been carrying a handbag. Keys and things came out to fall to the floor and like before, her wedding ring and engagement ring were pulled from her finger before she was lifted up and thrown over for the five hundred foot drop down into the gorge below.

Retrieving everything, the assailant then silently disappeared into the darkness and next day, another suitcase was removed from its depository to be added to the other two in another one.

The body in the ravine wasn't found for four days. It had only been spotted by chance by some ramblers that had paused on the viaduct to look at the scenery when foxes were seen below. They were noticed because they are known to be nocturnal scavengers and it was of much interest to see them in broad daylight. It was soon apparent that what they were chewing and fighting over was a human body.

It was both a hazardous operation as well as being a grisly one for the people who had the task of retrieving the body from the gorge. Four days at the mercy of foxes as well as other animals, it was hardly recognisable as being human. The face, hands, feet and the internal organs had been torn from the body and even the pathologist was revolted at what was presented to him.

An open verdict was given and the body finished up in the morgue as an unidentified female. Before this happened, the next day after the death of this woman, another phone call was made.

'I can't stand much more of this,' the hysterical voice over the phone blurted out when the receiver was picked up. 'I've moved from hotel to hotel in London for I know they're onto me.'

'Who?'

'I don't know,' she wailed. 'You're the only one I've been able to contact. Please come and get me. Wear the Parisian scarf so that I will recognise you.' It was a heartfelt plea that she just had to respond to and noted down the hotel in North London and immediately put her outer coat on and with the head scarf as requested, set off.

The hotel itself had been carefully reconnoitred, one of many over several weeks to find a means of what was about to happen. It was an old, early Victorian mansion that had been converted into a hotel. The huge room had been subdivided into single rooms, it being made clear by the fact of the ceiling rose that had been the centerpiece of a hanging chandelier was no longer in the middle of the room but off to one side. It was this that had attracted her attention for the hook that had held the long lost chandelier was still in place.

She had booked into this room having surveyed them over a period of weeks, the day before she made the phone call. Now with her third victim on the way made her preparations. A chair was placed under this hook and one end of a Parisian scarf was tied to the hook and pulled until it was tight and taut. With a small sharp knife this was then frayed close up to the hook until it parted. A noose was now fashioned of the other end and put to one side with a screwdriver pushed through the knot before she sat down to wait for her visitor to arrive. She had been given the room number and told not to stop at the desk but come straight up to the room where her killer waited.

She was very calm as she sat there and waited for nearly two hours before there came a tentative knock at the door. She quickly got up and went and opened it and hustled the visitor inside.

'Thank God you came,' she said, pushing her into the room in front of her.

'Now what's all this cloak and dagger stuff about?' the visitor asked as she took off her scarf only to have the other one with the noose be slipped over her head. She didn't say any more for the tightening noose cut off her vocal cords as the screwdriver was twisted and she was pushed in the middle of her back, driving her down onto her knees.

Then with the other woman behind and on top, bore her down onto the carpet as the tourniquet was tightened and tightened with every twist of the screwdriver, choking and rupturing the muscles of her neck. She struggled as her face was pushed down to the carpet, her fingers clawed at the carpet as her life was choked out of her with the knee of her assailant in the middle of her back as the noose strangled her.

The killer stayed on her back for a full five minutes before moving off and checking for a pulse. Without finding one, she finally pulled the screwdriver out of the knot and after putting it in her pocket, pulled the dead body beneath the ceiling rose that had the other end of the scarf still attached to it.

The only chair in the room was knocked over and then with a piece of stationery paper from a drawer placed on the floor, then carefully with a toothpick she cleaned the nails of the victim that had clawed at the carpet. The miniscule and invisible fibres were cleaned from the nails onto the paper that was then carefully folded and put into her coat pocket.

Standing back to survey the scene, she scuffed the carpet where the fingers had been and satisfied, put on the wig from the drawer and donned her own Parisian head scarf and left the room, quietly shutting the door behind her.

***

THE PHONE in the car bleeped and the passenger picked up the handset and triggered the call.

'Moss.'

'Er, sorry to bother you sir, but I knew you was in Camden and thought you might like to just check in with a reported suicide up there.' the call had come through from the response officer in Scotland yard. Detective Inspector Moss with Detective Constable Twist driving, had just finished visiting the site of a warehouse break-in and were on their way back to the yard.

'Okay,' he sighed. 'Give me the address.' He repeated the location for the benefit of Twist who turned at the next corner and they pulled up outside the hotel two minutes later.

'Bloody hell, that was quick,' said the Medical examiner coming over and stopping by the car as Moss and Twist got out. 'I was expecting one of the nerds, not *the* top one.'

'We try to be of service however low the crime,' Moss replied.

'Crime? It's a suicide,' the examiner said.

'How astute of you to ascertain that without seeing the body,' Moss replied and only got a grunt to that response as they went into the hotel. The manager was there, wringing his hands and quickly showed them up to the room.

'Who else has been in the room?' Moss asked of the manager.

'No one sir, except the maid who found the body,' he answered.

'Is she still here?'

'Yes sir. We didn't move her.'

'The maid I meant!'

'Yes sir, an' a right state she's in.'

'Get a statement later, Twist,' Moss said as they went into the room. The medical examiner knelt down by the body and felt at the neck for a pulse first before putting the palm of his hand flat on her bare arm. He'd noted the knotted scarf round her neck and also the frayed end that he held in his hand, glancing up at the ceiling to see the other end tied up to the hook. Moss had also noted the last two facts.

'Dead,' the examiner said laconically. 'Rough guess, twelve hours. Know more after an autopsy.'

'Okay, Twist. Get a statement from the maid,' he said as his eyes swept round the room. Bed not slept in, no sign of any luggage nor of a handbag. Did she just walk in and hang herself? He opened the small wardrobe to find it empty as were all the drawers in the room, nothing. He went out and downstairs to speak to the manager.

'Can I see the register?' he asked and turned the book round before it was offered. 'When did she book in?' he asked as he scanned down the page till he found the room number against her name.

'Yesterday. Yesterday afternoon. I signed her in.'

'Miss or Mrs., for the name is illegible.' Moss had noticed that she hadn't been wearing any rings on her left hand, but that didn't mean a thing nowadays.

'I don't know sir,' he said, wringing his hands again.

'Did she have any baggage?'

'No sir. We get many people who when only staying for one night don't have any luggage.'

'Was she a hooker?'

'I don't know. I've never seen her before.'

'How did she pay? Cash, cheque, credit card?'

'Cash sir.' Moss sighed at this. No luggage, pays cash, probably a false name, the hall marks of a suicide.

'Okay. The room's to stay sealed until forensics have been over it. Twist!' he called out and the constable, his sidekick came over. 'Get onto forensics to check the room out, prints and all the rest.'

'Yes sir,' he said and pulled his mobile out of his pocket and got onto control.

The ambulance men came into the hotel's small lobby then and stopped when they saw Moss. The medical examiner came down the stairs and went over to Moss.

'Can they take her away, I've finished here?' he asked. Moss waved his hand in assent.

'Let me know the result of your probing,' Moss said as he signaled to Twist to follow him.

'We've got better things to do than suicides,' he said to Twist when they got back into the car, and yet, he had this nagging feeling inside of him about this and pushed it to the back of his mind to wait until he had the autopsy report.

This took two days to land on his desk and cutting through the medical jargon, it said the woman had died of strangulation consistent with an attempted hanging. But still he had this nagging doubt. He'd seen something there in that room but couldn't put his finger on what it was that was making him uncomfortable about the report.

It was another two days and Moss was just trying to finish off his report of a warehouse break-in when he knew he was missing one statement.

'Where's that security guard's statement?' he asked Twist.

'Here. I haven't finished my notes to go with it,' he said.

'Well how long is it going to take?'

'How long's a piece of string?' Twist fired back at him.

How long is a piece of string! How long is a piece of cloth and he knew then what had been bothering him.

'Saunders!' he roared out and the heads of people at other desks reared up at his bellow. One young WPC got up and almost ran to where he was sitting.

'How tall are you?' he barked out.

'Er…er…five foot eight sir,' Woman Police Constable Rachel Saunders stammered out. Moss flipped open the file on the suicide and noted that she was five foot nine.

'Twist!' he shouted out again.

'Yes sir?' he replied, only sitting one desk away.

'Get that scarf of the suicide and meet me down at the car. You,' he said to Saunders, 'come with me.' he strode out of the large room with WPC Saunders following him as Twist went off to find the scarf that his boss wanted.

Moss was sitting in the front seat of the car with Saunders in the back, his fingers drumming on the dash as Twist came hurrying out of the building and got into the driving seat. Moss took the scarf and passed it back to Saunders.

'The hotel in Camden,' he ordered, and sat back as Twist drove out of the yard and went North.

Thirty minutes later, the three of them entered the hotel. The room had been reopened but it didn't stop Moss from getting the room opened.

'Out!' he said to the manager and shut the door behind him. 'Now get that chair Twist and place it underneath that hook in the ceiling.' He did as he was told.

'Okay Saunders, the scarf,' and he held out his hand and took it from hers and alarmed her when he placed the noose of it, for it was still knotted as it was found, round her neck. 'Now get up onto the chair. Help her, Twist.' He did by taking hold of her arm and helped her to stand up on the chair.

'Now Saunders, take the free end and reach up to the hook. Up as far as you can reach.' She did as she was told and only then did Twist give a gasp for he realised what his governor had spotted and he hadn't, for with Saunders being of a comparable height to the suicide, there was no way she could have reached the hook in the ceiling. Her arm was outstretched with the frayed end in her hand but she was still a good twelve inches short.

'How long is a piece of string,' Moss muttered. 'twelve inches too short. Thank you Saunders, you can get down now. Twist, we have a murder on our hands!'

***

MOSS SAT at his desk and quickly wrote out a one page report and took it along to the Chief Superintendent.

'Yes, I agree, it does appear to be murder. Okay. You handle it with Twist and you can have four WPC's and two constables.' the Superintendent said.

'Six? I need at least ten sir,' Moss said.

'Six is all I can spare. You'll just have to make do.'

'Yes sir,' Moss said a little sullenly and left the office.

'Saunders!' he called out when at his office door.

'Yes sir,' she said as she hurried up to him.

'Find three other loose women and meet me in the incident room. Twist! Get two other constables. Not Perkins.'

'Perkins has been returned to uniform duties sir,' Twist replied.

'Thank God for that. Round up two, incident room,' he said as he went into his office and picked up the autopsy report along with his own and went to where he would be working on this case. In the incident room, he pinned up two photos of the dead women and wrote on the board the name and address of the hotel in Camden as people began to file into the room. He waited until they were all in the room before closing the door.

'From an apparent suicide we've moved on to a murder,' he began. 'A white Caucasian female. Mid to late twenties, early thirties. That's all we have apart from her fingerprints. Twist, you check these to see if she has a record, and teeth. Saunders. Get copies made of the dental chart from the autopsy report and pass them round. I want these checked with every dentist in London.'

'Do you know how many dentists there are in London, sir?' a constable asked.

'No Trevis, but I'm sure you're about to tell me,' he said in a honeyed tone.

'There's at least five thousand if not more. If they all have just two hundred patients, that's a million people, sir.'

'Well you can halve that because of males and halve it again for the women because of the age. So you are only looking at a quarter of a million. Also judging by the influx of foreign nationals, the total count will be far less. Three fillings will make it easier even more, so the sooner you divide up the city and check, the sooner it will be done.'

'So sayeth the Lord,' Trevis muttered low so that Moss couldn't hear but those closest to him chuckled.

'Could we also have a photo fit to show,' one WPC asked. 'That might speed things up too, sir.'

'Right Wright. Get hold of the police artist and pop along to the morgue. Tomkins. You can go to the hotel and get another statement from the manager. I want as accurate a description you can get of the woman who checked in for I feel that this was the murderer, luring her victim to the hotel. Wallis?'

'Yes sir?' a WPC answered.

'Check missing persons. Right, that will keep you all busy for a day or two, get going,' and so they all filed out to begin the task of finding out the name of the murdered woman.

Moss went back to his office to clear up as much of the backlog of previous reports before he began to get facts on this present case.

**

THE FACTS that had turned up in the first two weeks showed that the dead woman didn't have a police record according to the fingerprint department. She had not been reported missing and neither had her teeth revealed any dentist so far that might have treated her. The photo fit hadn't produced anybody recognising her and the hotel manager swore that the drawing was like the woman who had checked into his hotel.

It was very frustrating for Moss and the team and he eventually resorted to having the photo fit published in the national papers asking if anyone recognised her. To this, they began to get reports and it didn't make sense with the locations being so varied. Norfolk, Surrey, Yorkshire, Devon and many places in between.

They all had to be checked out which in itself was no mean task, with the squad travelling all over England to interview the people who had reported in. In the incident room, a map of the country had been put up and these sightings marked and as the reports began to filter back, a pattern began to emerge. The pattern was racecourses and the surname of Pound kept recurring. The wife of a bookmaker.

There was excitement in the incident room for it only took a phone call to the Bookmakers Association to get the name of Michael Pound with his address in Bagshot. This also tied up with three reports from that area and so Moss, Twist and Saunders got a car out and went to visit the address.

It didn't take them long to get to the house and found that it was empty, no response to their knocking or ringing of the doorbell. Moss had no compunction at having Twist break a window for them to get access to the inside. The photographs on a sideboard confirmed that they were in the right place. They took a quick look through drawers and found her name as being Jane Pound. Twist had been over the house and declared that it didn't appear to have been in use for some time. Saunders confirmed this by the state of the inside of the fridge in the kitchen.

Moss phoned the yard and had a forensic team dispatched immediately and two hours later, had a match of the fingerprints, but nothing else of value to them was turned up while they were there. Moss had Twist and Saunders gather up all papers and contents of desk drawers as well as those of the bedside cabinets for closer examination back at the station. The desks in the incident room were cleared and the contents of the three large boxes were minutely scrutinized. Every letter, memo or note were read and sorted into different piles.

'Sir,' Saunders interrupted Moss. 'It seems that Mr. Pound died as result of an accident and Mrs. Pound received just short of half a million pounds insurance money. Now this surely would have been paid into her bank, but I cannot find one bank statement that belonged to her in this lot.'

'Very good, Saunders. Get onto the banks in Bagshot and find which one she used and then get them to fax over her statements for the past two years.'

'Yes sir,' she said and went off to this task.

Two hours later, she placed a bunch of faxes on his desk.

'Well, well,' he murmured as he quickly scanned through them before passing over one to Twist. 'She drew the lot out over a three-week period and we didn't find any in the house. Wallis! Wright! Tomkins and Nichols! I want you to go to the house and tear it apart. Find the money.'

The four looked at each and shrugged their shoulders and left the room to do as they had been instructed.

'Find the money and you've found the murderer,' he said to Saunders.

***

THEY FOUND nothing after two days of searching the house. Then came the painstaking task of interviewing all known associates of the Pounds and checking their alibis for the day and night of the murder. Again, nothing. Other banks over a wide area were asked if large sums had been paid in totaling nearly half a million pounds without any result. Safe deposit boxes rented from the date of her receiving the insurance money till her death were checked. No joy there either.

'Where would you hide the money and why?' was the question Moss kept asking himself as well as Twist and Saunders. The 'where' part of the question came to him when they were driving through an in-dustrial estate a couple of days later. Well it was a possibility, he thought, and had Twist drive back to the yard and get a search warrant for storage depots.

'Get a dozen with the locations blank,' he instructed him and he gathered the team together and split them up into pairs. Saunders was given the task of finding the locations in London and splitting them up for the teams to search.

'We are not looking into every locker in these places but the smallest. Those that have been rented over the past year. I would think that we are looking for a large briefcase, suitcase or box with money in it. Then get the name and address of whoever rented it. It will probably be false but we must still check them out.'

Twist returned with the warrants and Saunders gave out a printed list to each team and sent them off. It took them two days to check each one on the list and when they gathered again in the incident room, Moss had each of them report what they had found.

'We found four that had been rented in this time period. Two were full up and two were empty,' WPC Wallis said, handing over her list to him.

'We found six,' Pc Tomkins said. 'Five full up and one empty.' He too passed over his list. The third list was passed over to add to his one and it was very clear that four of the empty ones had been rented by the same person, Ruth Roberts, with the same address given.

'Well done, everyone. Twist, Saunders, let us pay a visit on this Ruth Roberts.' The three of them left and were soon in a car heading for Chelsea. They had no response to ringing any of the four bells to the flats and Twist had observed that the door looked too solid to break into.

'Then we'll ask the estate agent to let us in,' Moss said, pointing to the sign fixed to the railings by the front gate.

The manager of the estate agent was most helpful when shown the warrant card of Moss. He confirmed by looking through their files that a Ruth Roberts had flat number three at that address and went with them in his own car back to the flat with his spare sets of keys. The flat had that stale smell of not being used very often and also that it hadn't been used for some time.

'Bingo!' came the cry from Saunders when she opened a wardrobe and moved aside for Moss to look inside.

'Four cases?' he said. 'One would have been enough.'

He noted a dark top coat hanging up inside and gently turned it on its hanger and knew that he was now well on the way to solving his case, for there, wrapped under the coat was a silk scarf, exactly like the one that had been round the victim's throat.

'Get forensics down here immediately,' he said to Twist who used his phone to send for them. 'Mr. Forbes,' this being the estate office manager, 'the keys please. This flat is now part of a murder investigation. They will be returned to you when we have completed our examination. Twist, go back with him and get a statement from whoever had dealings with this Roberts woman.' The two left and Moss and Saunders waited for the forensic team to dust the suitcases for prints before he could open them.

These were the first things to be treated and they lifted six sets from the four suitcases before going over the flat to find more that they could try to match up later.

'Okay, let's see what's in the first one,' Moss said as he pulled it out and put it on the bed and opened it.

'Bingo,' Saunders said again when they saw that it was half full of money, most of it still banded. He didn't touch any of it for he wanted prints lifted off the bundles as well. 'The others must be clothes then,' Saunders said as he heaved out the second one.

'Wow,' she gasped when it was opened to reveal it full of money, more than what was in the first one.

'Oh shit!' Moss breathed out when the fourth one was opened to reveal it too held money. 'I should have guessed with four lockups. There's more here than there should be. Saunders! Back to the office. I want you to phone every insurance company you can think of to find out if over the past six to nine months they have made out any large payments and to whom. I'm looking for another three names,' he finished grimly.

By the end of the normal working day, five o'clock to most office workers, they had the three names. Robert Seymour of Berkshire, died in a hit and run. Wife, Anne, was the recipient of his insurance pay out. Stephen Mann from Malden, Essex, drowned. His wife, Francis, paid. William Swithers, London, died in an underground accident. Wife Penelope was paid out.

'Saunders. I want an arrest warrant for the murder of Jane Pound made out to Ruth Roberts. I also want forensic teams to go over the three addresses to see what they come up with apart from fingerprints. I want the counties concerned to let us know of any Jane Doe's they have and also their fingerprints.'

'You think all four of them?' she asked.

'Yes, I'm afraid so.' She went off to her tasks and he went along to his Superintendent to report what he had uncovered so far.

'Excellent Moss, and your conclusions?' he'd asked.

'That all four men were murdered for the insurance money and not accidents as recorded. Then all four women have been murdered by this Ruth Roberts who must have master minded the whole thing. I'm just about to issue an all-points bulletin to arrest and hold her at all air and sea ports and for us to be informed if they do so,' he finished.

'Well done Moss, carry on'' the Superintendent said.

***

IT WAS the forensic teams that pointed the way to the killer by the means of the fingerprints. Those on the suitcases matched those taken from the four homes. They would also be able to identify the money by taking fingerprints of various bank employees that would have handled it. One set gave them a name to one Jane Doe because they matched but where forensic came up trumps was with the coat taken from the flat of Roberts. They found carpet fibres wrapped in paper that when checked, matched those of the carpet in the hotel room in Camden. Also, there were only one set of prints on the paper which pointed out the killer.

'Sir,' Saunders called out, waving her hand. 'I've got a check-in desk at Heathrow. A Ruth Roberts has just checked into the First Class lounge.'

'Nichols! Take over that phone and get through to air traffic control to delay that plane. Twist, Saunders, come with me,' he cried as he rushed out of the incident room, those two hurrying to keep up with him.

Twist drove with the siren going as they raced through London to get onto the M4. Saunders was on the phone to the airport security for one man to be waiting for them at the departure entrance to look after the car when they arrived. The siren was only turned off when they entered the tunnel at the approach to the airport and came to a halt outside the departure entrance where a security guard was waiting for them.

Moss led the way through the milling throng till they reached the British Airways flight checking-in desk for the First Class section. He showed the girl his warrant card and she said that it was her who'd phoned in.

'She's in the lounge,' she said as she began to lead them there.

'How did you pick it up,' Moss asked her as they moved along, 'when passport control didn't?'

'Coincidence really. The name stuck in my mind because it's the same as my mother's maiden name,' she said as they reached the door to the lounge. 'There. The woman facing the windows.'

Moss strode over, flanked by Twist and Saunders and went and stood in front of her. He recognised her from pictures in her house.

'I'm arresting you, Ruth Roberts, for the murder of one Jane Pound, though rather than calling you by the false name, I should use your real name – Mrs. Penelope Swithers.'

THE END

Here is a sample from another story you may enjoy:

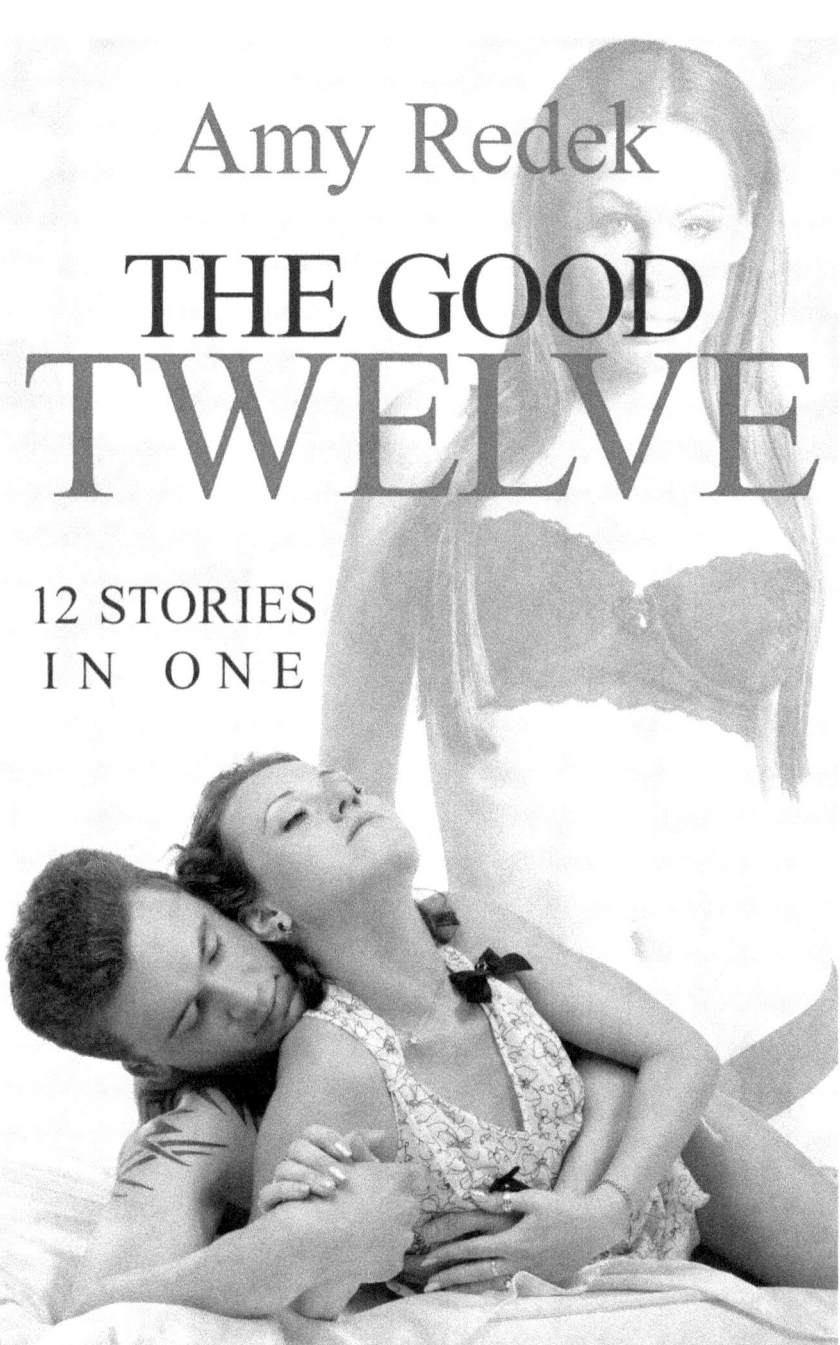

Amy Redek

THE GOOD
TWELVE

12 STORIES
IN ONE

I was orphaned at an early age and was most fortunate to be taken in by Peter and Mary Withers, for I took the place of the child they never had.

Peter was the gamekeeper for Lord Carlton on his estate in Wiltshire and Mary helped out in the house when they had guests, which was mostly in the shooting season. We lived in the lodge at the entrance to the estate and were about a mile from the small village down the lane.

I was happy there as I grew up and Peter saw to my schooling for there was nowhere else I could go for this. Being the gamekeeper, he knew all about animals and birds that lived out in the woods and fields and when I went out with him, he would point out the different species and how to track them. Though part of his job was to keep the poachers at bay and stop them from snaring the pheasants and grouse.

It was some years before he would take me out with him on his nightly prowls, moving quietly to try and find traps that the poachers would set up in the woods. I got to learn the most likely places they would be set and I was quite pleased when I did find one.

'Well done Tom,' he would cry and ruffle the hair of my head, a habit of his for I was far shorter than he was.

One of the turning points of my life was when I was allowed to go into the pub with him. I'd been refused entry before because I was too small but now that I was growing up, they turned a blind eye to me going in with him as long as I behaved myself.

I used to like those evenings, though it was only twice a week. We'd have our dinner and then we'd set off for the pub in the village which was a good mile down the lane. It was only a small place, but now that I was older, they let me in and it was Old Percy who bought me my first beer. It was only half a pint of bitter, but it made the night for me to drink with the locals.

Peter and I would settle ourselves by the log fire and though I didn't smoke or wouldn't have been allowed to anyway, I did like the smell of his pipe when he lit it. He would stretch out his legs and puff away and I would stretch my feet out too and listen to the older men talk.

Though most of what they talked about went over my head and after drinking my small half pint of beer, I would drowse in front of the fire only catching half of what they said. Peter would have maybe three pints but drew the line with me, saying that half was enough. In spite of this restriction on my drinking, I still enjoyed those evenings.

Come ten o'clock, he would finish his beer and wake me up and tell me it was time for bed and that I couldn't sleep in the pub. We would then walk the mile back home and invariable, Mary would be in bed but she always left us a little something to eat before we went to bed. I think she would have been annoyed if she knew that Peter was letting me drink beer when I was out with him.

If you enjoyed this sample then look for **The Good Twelve**.

Also by this Author:

The Painted Sword

Cruise Control

Wild Pleasures

Lending My Beloved

Lady of Cuckolds

Lady of Pleasure

Lady Magenta

Sexually Overdosed

Meeting My Fancy Dear

Prison Sex Slave

Chasing A Shadow

The Hostel

The Island

Thirst for Drugs and Pleasure

Forgotten Identity

Grey Memories

Chronos: Time Machine

The Hard Bomber

Honeymoon Abduction

The Yacht Sins

Summer at the Villa

Practice Makes Perfect

Stranger Danger

Following Father's Footsteps

The Square Circle

The Wizard of Kos

Coming Together

Out in the Real World

Me, Carol and Raoul

Under the Mistletoe

Play House

A Cocktale for Sherry

Loving Rhett

Farell

Homos Ubique

Foxhole

Deaf, Dumb and Blind

Loving the Mechanic

Up for Sale

No White Snow

Love Motel

A Man's Toy

From the Author

WANT FREE COPIES OF MY BOOKS?
Just visit my blog and download free copies of my books:
amy-redek.awesomeauthors.org/amy-redek

Author Central – http://www.amazon.com/Amy-Redek/e/B00A48NQ72

If you enjoyed any of my books then please share the love and click like on my books in Amazon.

If you write me a review and send me an email I will send you a free book, or many.
(Just know that these emails are filtered by my publisher.)

Good news is always welcome.

One Last Thing, For Kindle Readers...

When you turn the page, Kindle will give you the opportunity to rate this book and share your thoughts on Facebook and Twitter. If you enjoyed my writings, would you please take a few seconds to let your friends know about it? Because... when they enjoy they will be grateful to you and so will I.

Thank You!

Amy Redek
amy_redek@awesomeauthors.org

About the Author

George Eliot was a famous writer, though at the time, only male authors were recognised. It was in fact the pen name of Mary Ann Evans, a female.

When I started writing, I thought that if a woman could use a male name, why, with me being male, why couldn't I use the name of a female? Though to be different, I made my writer's name from an anagram of my real name.

I wasn't the brightest spark in my school days and it was only while being in the Merchant Navy did I self-educate myself. That being mostly literature, classical music and artists, like Tolstoy, Chopin and Rembrandt. After leaving the navy, I had several jobs, finishing up by being a working boss using my own maxim that 'Management is the art of delegation.'

It's when I became self-employed that I began to write, though sadly, not many of my books can be published because of certain laws that forbid certain aspects of life. This never fazed me for I was really writing just to please myself having a wide range of the human psych.

Having written ninety stories, my only aim now is to reach one hundred. I give thanks to the publishers for at least putting some of my efforts out for others to enjoy as much as I did in the writing of them.

You may also like the books by these authors:

Nicki Homewood

The Debtor's Performance

Exhibitionist Erotica

I sat at the table and prayed for a number higher than eight. The dice felt warm in my sweaty hand and I could feel my heart pounding in my chest. They rolled round inside my hand and I scattered them down the table, closing my eyes at the final moment of ejection as they made their way down the table and settled.

I let my head fall backwards, tried to relax my neck, feeling my rich golden hair fall down my back, hoping against hope that finally my luck had changed. I heard the girl next to me gasp and I tried to determine what that meant for me. Had I won at last?

Three and Two.

Not enough, not nearly enough.

What would happen next, I wondered. I was so far beyond the limit of credit that I had initially agreed that I could not believe they would let me borrow more. My credit cards were already maxed out and however good a customer I was, I couldn't believe that they would let me keep on playing. I had already had an interview with Mr Abadlioi last week after the previous set of losses.

I looked down at the beautiful blue satin dress that I was wearing. I had picked it out because the last time I had worn it, I had been lucky, had come away better than level. I loved the big slit down the front, the way that it showed off so much of my cleavage. Around the casino there were certain rules of behaviour that I loved. Guys could admire a beautiful woman and women could be admired, but no one would make much of a move, no one would hassle you. It was nice, and safe.

Economically it was not safe, I reflected. Economically it was a disaster, a life-changing, misery-inducing, marriage-destroying disaster.

I could feel my string pulling into my ass a little, the tops of my stockings on my hips, the lace gently hugging me to keep themselves in place. The satin was smooth and sexy against my skin and I thought that I may never be able to afford to buy such a garment again.

Silence descended over the table as behind me I could hear a group of people approaching me. I turned slowly with a forced smile on my lips.

"Mrs DiAngelo, perhaps I could suggest that you come this way," Mr Abadlioi asked, a cold politeness still evident in his voice.

Behind him were two guys, not goons exactly but big guys that could look after themselves in a fight I was sure. Not that fighting was exactly my thing.

We walked away from the table and I could feel the eyes of all the people on the floor track me as I walked out past the tables, past the fruit machines and down a darker corridor leading to the backrooms where the reality of casino debts started to encroach on real life. No longer here were you just dealing in coloured plastic chips, this was where cheques and credit cards lived, and debt collectors and lawyers I supposed.

The guys on either side of me didn't even look at me. Here I was wearing a practically skin tight satin dress, pulled tight over my tits, accentuating my 34B breasts that were otherwise unencumbered with cover or support. I knew that men found this dress very sexy. I had seen the looks of lust, of desire in their eyes many times. I knew that my husband loved to see me in it, loved to see the way it showed the lines of my firm breasts, and just gave away a little of my nipples as they pressed into the fabric.

I was shown once again into his office and sat down opposite him, ensconced behind his huge solid oak desk. He smiled at me graciously.

"Well, Mrs DiAngelo, we seem to find ourselves here again. Well, well, well. And so soon," he started.

"I seem to be going through a very unlucky run," I mumbled nervously.

"Yes, well that is certainly clear. But the problem for me is now really just how we are going to recover the funds. I seem to remember last time that you were very keen to keep it between the two of us. Does that remain the case?" he asked, his eyes roaming down over my form.

If you enjoyed this sample then look for **The Debtor's Performance.**

Just Plain Bob

Cyndi

Intense Erotica

My sister was getting married and I had to fly back to Michigan for the wedding. I was running a little late for the flight and I didn't have time to stop and browse the magazine rack for something to read on the flight. Once we were airborne, I checked the seat pockets on my row and I found a well-thumbed copy of Gallery magazine. I ended up reading it from cover to cover, but what grabbed me was the section called Feedback. It had half a dozen letters from guys who got turned on from watching their wives get it on with other men. One in particular really got to me, it was from a guy who set up gangbangs for his wife and then ate her out after all the guys were done with her. The eating her out part didn't appeal to me, but I started having thoughts about what my sexy wife would look like in the throes of passion being serviced by other guys. The idea turned me on so much that my dick stayed hard the entire flight to Detroit.

Luckily, Cyndi had flown back a couple of days ahead of me and was going to be meeting my flight; and considering how hard my dick was, I was seriously considering that we might just have to get it on in the car in the parking lot. Any thoughts of having Cyndi take care of my problem died as I came down the ramp and saw her waiting for me with my mother and sister. We did get it on later that night, but with nowhere near the intensity that would have been there just after the flight.

***

As charged up as I was after reading that copy of Gallery, it all faded during the hectic week that followed and it wasn't until the flight home that the charge built up again. This time I was early for the flight and as I checked out the magazine racks at the terminal I spotted the latest issue of Gallery and I bought it. I also noticed a magazine that had "Hot Wives" on the cover and I bought it too. It turned out to be Penthouse Letters and it was even hotter than the first Gallery that I had read. My wife, who was traveling with me this time, had occasion to reach across me for something and her wrist hit my erection. She stopped and cupped my hard cock with her hand and smiled:

"Is that for me?"

"As soon as we get home my sweet, just as soon as we get home."

She gave me a squeeze and asked me what caused it and I showed her the cover of the magazine I was reading.

"I want to read it when you get done. If it does this," and she gave me another squeeze, "for you, I wonder what it will do for me."

I know what I'm hoping it will do, I thought. I passed her the Penthouse when I was done and I picked up the Gallery, and as I read it, I kept glancing at Cyndi out of the corner of my eye to see how she was reacting. All I saw was concentration and she never once betrayed what she might be thinking.

On the ride home from the airport, Cyndi was not her usual talkative self and I commented on it. She gave me a look that I couldn't decipher and said:

"I'm sitting here wondering if I should be worrying about you, or maybe more to the point, worrying about us."

"In what way?" I asked.

"Well, you got a hard-on from reading that magazine, but when I read it all, I found there were sections on anal sex, domination, homosexuality, swinging and swapping and one on watching your wife have sex with other men. The section on anal sex shouldn't have much of an effect on you because we have practiced anal sex since we started dating. That leaves the other four and if one of those excites you then we have a problem because all of them leave me cold."

Discretion being the better part of valor, I lied.

If you enjoyed this sample then look for **Cyndi**.

JACK RYDER

THE CHEATING GAME

NAUGHTY EROTICA

I can't really remember exactly how I came up with the idea. The WHY is as clear as day, even after all these years. The entire motivation behind my sly little plan was driven by a deep rage fueled lust to get even with a malicious infidelity and to fulfill a childhood fantasy. I had fantasized about my sexy MILF mother-in-law ever since I started dating her daughter way back in high school. I had been leery of my best friend Peter's lust for my wife almost nearly as long. It would ultimately be those two things thrown together by circumstance, that would drive me to make the plan and take the actions that I have.

But I am getting way ahead of myself here. I should start at the beginning, so you may understand why this happened and maybe you won't hate me in the end. It's not like I ruined anyone's life or physically hurt anyone. Although I manipulated some situations, I did not force anyone to do the things they did all by themselves willingly. Although I started some wheels in motion, the results found a momentum of their own. The bottom line is that cheaters cheat and I took full advantage of that.

I would have to say that the event that started the ball rolling, happened the night of my bachelor party. It wasn't a surprise to anyone that Nikki and I were gonna tie the knot. We have been inseparable since we first met on the first day of high school. My best friend Pete has been the only other significant person that has been part of the last three years of our lives, along with Nikki's mom Krysta.

Nikki and I wanted to get married right after graduation, so we would have some time together before she travelled across the state to attend college. We knew the distance would keep us apart for certain amounts of time, but we were both determined to continue our plans so we could build a successful life together. I would stay home and continue working, so I could take over my father's company someday. Nikki would complete her education and someday become my accountant. We had a plan and we were certain that we could make it work.

Pete insisted on throwing a big bachelor party. It was sort of embarrassing that most of the fellows that attended that night were really Pete's friends. Although I knew most of the fellows, they were just mostly acquaintances from various school functions. I had asked Pete to keep the party a low key event, but he went all out anyway. It was my initial feeling that Pete just wanted to seem like a big shot to all his other buddies. It wouldn't be till some time later, that he had an entirely different motive.

It was really your average rented bar sort of bachelor party. Complete with strippers, lap dancers, and a lot of liquor consumption. I was pleased that he had at least thought ahead enough to contact a shuttle bus taxi service to get everyone home safely. I made it a point to not get nearly as drunk as the rest of the fellows. But it seemed like Pete was trying his best to force more drinks on my way even if I left them untouched.

Throughout the evening, each of the strippers made their way over to kiss and rub their mostly nude bodies all over the groom to be. It was very unsettling to me as the fellows took cell phone photos each time they did it. But I didn't make a big deal about it, since they were taking photos of all the girls rubbing all over the other fellows as well. I did notice that Pete seemed to get quite excited each time he took photos of the girls humping on me. He seemed to have a huge grin as he snapped his shots. Just before midnight, shortly after I told Pete I was about ready to go home, one of the strippers pushed me down onto my chair and proceeded to sit on my lap for a lap dance.

The fellows were all whooping and hollering, as she ripped off her top and shoved her big hooters in my face. When I saw the flashes from Pete's camera, I knew how this could look if Nikki ever saw them. As I grasped her hips to lift her off, her unfastened bikini bottom fell off and Pete snapped a photo with her nude body pressed against mine.

If you enjoyed this sample then look for **The Cheating Game**.

GEORGE X. BUSH

AFFAIRS
Conundrum
ATONEMENT
WIFE SHARING EROTICA

John Rutter approached his front door very weary from his day's work. A last-minute meeting had pushed his day into overtime and at 8pm he was just getting home. As he entered, he was surprised to hear voices from within as he set his briefcase down. Walking into the living room, he was even more surprised to see his boss, Horace Ender, and his wife, Emma, along with the ubiquitous presence of Horace's bodyguard/right-hand man, Jared, all 6'8" and 275 pounds of sculpted black imperviousness. Even more jarring was the presence of Horace's secretary, Melissa, a 5'4" red-headed pixie with an upturned, freckled nose beneath bright green eyes.

"So, you're finally home," Jean, John's wife said, pressing her body into his and kissing him lightly on the lips. "Busy day?" she asked, her bright green eyes staring into his as her braless breasts rubbed lightly against his chest, her waist-length blonde hair swaying back and forth.

"Very," John replied, still wondering how he could have forgotten that everyone was coming over this evening.

"Sorry to surprise you, John," Horace said, at 65 still a silver-haired, energetic powerhouse of a man whose 6'3" frame was dwarfed by the presence of Jared standing behind him.

"Not at all," John replied, nonplussed. "I thought I had forgotten you were coming or something."

"Hello, John," Emma said, her silvery-grey hair tied back in a ponytail just like her husband's. At 63 and 5'6", Emma Ender was still a beautiful, willowy woman with bright blue eyes. "Nice to see you again."

"Emma," John replied, taking her hand and kissing her on both cheeks. "My pleasure. You look great," he said, admiring her and her husband, both very tanned from spending so much time at their home in Hawaii. "To what do we owe the pleasure?" he asked.

"Your future, John," Horace replied, a firm look on his face.

"My future?" John said a bit nervously.

"Yes," Horace answered. "Why don't you sit down and we'll talk," he said, indicating the large seat next to him.

As John settled nervously into the seat, everyone else settled down, too, Jean sitting between Melissa and Emma on the sofa while Jared stood behind John imposingly.

"Now see here, John," Horace began. "As far as your work goes, I can't say we've ever had a better, more productive employee, so rest assured on that score."

"I'm happy to hear it," John replied.

"Your energy, innovative thinking, and enthusiasm have all combined to bring in much business," Horace said. "So naturally we think of promoting you. We like to keep the best and the brightest and most promising at all costs."

"Wow, I don't know what to say," John said, truly surprised that this moment had come after only 2 years with the company.

"But we also consider other factors," Horace continued, "in deciding which people are worth keeping, factors such as honesty, morality, and suitability to our particular type of corporate culture. Being a productive worker just isn't enough anymore in today's marketplace."

"I understand," John replied.

"We're interested in determining whether you're such a person," Horace said. "But we do have some reservations, I must admit, which is why we're here tonight."

"What do you mean?" John asked, struggling to keep the nervousness from his voice.

"Well, we like to know that managers in our company are honest, truthful, and can be relied upon at all times, as well as whether they fit into our particular corporate culture," Horace said. "Are you such a person, John? Are you honest and truthful? Do you fully fit into our particular type of corporate culture? Can you be relied upon at all times to do what is required of you and do so with the utmost in discretion? Now, think before you answer. This is extremely important. Everything about your future with the company depends upon how you respond this evening."

Everyone just watched John expectantly, saying nothing. The tension was so thick you could cut it with a knife.

"The best answer I can give you," John replied after due consideration, "is that I always try to be honest and truthful. I'm not a saint and I don't always succeed, but it's important to me, too, so I try. As for being reliable and acting with discretion as far as the company is concerned, 150%," he stated. "I have to say that I've never had a job that was as challenging, yet as exciting and fun. I look forward to going to work each and every day."

"Yes, that we're well aware of," Horace said somewhat cryptically. "But we're referring to your entire life when we talk about honesty and truthfulness and integrity, and even to an extent our particular corporate culture. Was your answer only about work or did it also cover your life in general?"

"My life, period," John answered without hesitation.

"I see," Horace said, a disturbed look on his face.

"John, when we got married, we agreed to always be open and honest with each other, to share our lives completely," Jean said from her seat on the sofa. "No matter what."

"That's right," John agreed, nodding his head warily.

"Neither of us were virgins when we met, but I've been absolutely faithful to you ever since we got married," she continued.

"Can you say the same, John?" Emma asked quietly from the sofa.

John just stared at the three of them sitting there, realizing suddenly that both Melissa and Emma were each holding one of Jean's hands.

"No," John replied quietly after a minute. "I can't say the same."

"I'm glad you're being honest with us, John," Horace said after a few moments of pregnant silence filled the room. "That's very important, believe me. Now, you're saying you've been unfaithful to your wife; is that correct?"

"Yes," John replied, hardly daring to look Jean in the face but not daring to look anywhere else.

"Has it been one woman, many women?" Horace asked.

"Just one," John answered.

"I see," Horace said, nodding his head. "And was this a one-time thing or an ongoing thing?"

"It's been ongoing," John admitted, hating the look of pain in Jean's eyes as she stared at him, white-knuckled as she held Melissa & Emma's hands.

"Are you in love with this other woman?" Horace asked.

"No," John answered, exhaling a huge breath. "It's just sex, lust."

"Your wife doesn't please you, satisfy you sexually enough?" Emma asked softly.

"Oh, no, it has nothing at all to do with Jean," John exclaimed. "I'm totally, 100% committed to her. I love her. Our sex life is good, great. I never leave the house without..." he said, then stopped as he realized he was saying too much.

"Without what?" Emma asked, a smile almost creasing her face.

"Without, without..." John tried to say.

"Without fucking me," Jean filled in. "And when he gets home, that's usually the first thing that happens, we fuck. That's why I don't understand..."

"And if saving your marriage and your job, depended upon you stopping this behavior immediately, would you? Could you?" Horace asked.

"Yes," John replied emphatically. "My marriage and job are far more important to me."

"And you'd be willing to atone for your transgressions if need be?" Horace asked.

"Yes, if that's what's necessary," John said, nodding his head, feeling the sweat on his brow even though it was a cool evening and the windows were open.

"How shall you atone?" Horace asked almost rhetorically. "Is it possible to atone for this?" he asked, reaching down and picking up the remote control and pointing it at the television and pushing a button.

John stared in astonishment as a side-by-side picture of his office appeared on the television, one view being from the door, the other from the wall behind his desk facing the door. No part of his office was hidden from view.

"Shall we get started," John's voice came from the television, followed almost immediately by John himself with Melissa trailing...

If you enjoyed this sample then look for <u>Affairs, Conundrum, Atonement</u>.

ABBY
CITY GIRL IN THE COUNTRY
EROTIC ROMANCE

KERRY JAMES

Abby had little difficulty in getting to this point, on the B3227 from Taunton heading towards South Molton, and guessed that somewhere on this road she should see a sign indicating her turn. Yet as she drove further and further into Devon she became uneasy that no such sign had revealed itself. Navigation became more of a problem as she drove deeper into the countryside, signposts, when you could find them; indicated a destination which then received no further mention at all upon succeeding signs. High banks on either side of the road meant that she had little clue as to where she was, the only point of reference was the ribbon of road unwinding ceaselessly and vanishing under the bonnet of her car and the occasional signs for some oddly named village or hamlet. As she passed through villages such as Wiveliscombe and Bampton, she wondered if she had gone wrong, and seeing the sign that said South Molton was just five miles farther on, decided that indeed she had gone wrong. Swearing mildly under her breath, Abby was giving thought to turning round and retracing her path.

Suddenly, she caught that breath; there was the sign. Leaning gently against the high banks that enclosed the road with a vigorous growth of Ivy as camouflage, she would have missed it had she not been driving slowly looking for a place to turn. It was a peculiar sensation, and her heart was beating furiously as she made the turn. A name that had previously existed only in hearsay and on a map was now a fact. Her mother had mentioned the name a few times without thinking, but would not be pressed on its significance. When her mother had died, Abby was nineteen, there was no reference at all to the name in her personal effects, which were few, there was no birth certificate, and the only official document she could find was an out of date passport, giving the birth area as South Molton. Abby's history consisted of just her mother's death certificates, and her own birth certificate. Abby now realised that she could have obtained a copy of her mother's birth certificate, but as is the way of things she had not thought logically at the time. She would repair this oversight as soon as possible. She wondered why her mum had a passport, as she had never travelled abroad.

Combe Linney, as Abby spelt it, was not even marked on her road map, and she had to resort to the Ordinance Survey to discover the location; again there was no place spelt Linney, but there was a Combe Lyney, near South Molton, and she assumed that this had to be the place. Its sum total consisted of two black oblongs, and a round dot with a cross on top, presumably indicating a church. There were no A or B roads that ventured anywhere near the place. If this wasn't the back of beyond, then it was pretty close to it.

The mystery could not be investigated immediately as Abby had after her mother's death, to consider the business of life, a job, somewhere to live. Her mother had left her little, but a stubborn trait that helped Abby survive the numerous jobs she took in the financial and insurance trade; making tea and coffee for surly men and women who viewed her simply as the office gofer.; They would have been surprised if they had known that Abby did not merely put their drinks in front of them, but closely studied what they were doing. They didn't know because Abby was invisible, unimportant, not even missed when she left to go to a better job, using all she had learned to pack her C.V. She was twenty-five when she started in the city as a proprietary equity trader, the years of watching and learning placed her in good stead. She would not say that she was a brilliant trader, there were many more that could turn sixpences into sovereigns at the drop of a hat, but she was intuitive, and with no family to call upon her time, was content to work all hours to achieve her goal. In a business where employers counted the hours almost as important as the success, she was regarded highly.

If you enjoyed this sample then look for <u>Abby</u>.

WANT FREE COPIES OF MY BOOKS?

Just visit my blog and download free copies of my books:
amy-redek.awesomeauthors.org/amy-redek